ENEMY EX'S SECRET BABY

CALLIE STEVENS

PROLOGUE

AXEL

Seven years ago

"Are you cold?" I ask as I softly run my finger down Gillian's arm. Her skin is so warm, yet covered in goosebumps.

"Excited," she says. And my body immediately responds to the husky tone of her voice.

How is it that a single word from her has the power to bring me to my knees?

She takes my hand from her arm and guides it to her breast, bending my fingers around the plump flesh. "Did you think about me?"

There was nothing else I could think about. But all I say is, "Yes."

"I thought about you too," she lets me know. And I'm powerless to continue resisting her.

I dip my head and cover her lips with mine. As our mouths meet, heat explodes inside me.

The sounds of the beach are swirling around us as birds

caw, water laps at the shore, an easy sea breeze runs by, but all I can feel is her. This girl is my whole world, and that scares the hell out of me.

I know I have to let her go sooner rather than later, but this here is something I can't fight.

We lay on the sand and our hands take over, exploring every inch possible. Soon, the clothes between us become a prison and we can't take them off fast enough.

I need to feel her against me, skin on skin. Her heat against mine. Her softness against my hardness.

I lay our clothes down as a makeshift blanket, because... sand. Not fun.

As soon as I'm done, I lay her down and devour her, first with my eyes, then my hands and mouth.

When she finally finds her release, I climb up her body, kissing, licking, and nipping as I go, and I get situated, between her legs. If I don't get inside her fast, I might explode.

As she closes her legs around me, our pelvises lock into place, my cock slipping inside her tight, warm pussy.

Heaven on earth. Home.

I start thrusting slowly. In and out. Enjoying the feel of her wet folds around me. She feels so good it's a struggle to hold myself back.

"Oh god, Axel. Feels so good."

"So good, baby." I kiss her mouth and let me mouth trail down her jawline to her collarbone.

"More, I need more."

I'm making love to her and I want this to last. I want to enjoy her. But I can't not give her what she needs, so I thrust a little harder, just to give her some more friction. That little extra something to drive her crazy.

God, she feels amazing and I'm holding myself back

with all my might. I want to claim her. Own her. Ruin her for all men.

"Axel, please. I need you."

"What do you need, baby?" I'll give her anything. The world and the moon. I'd give her my whole life if I could.

"Everything. Make me yours."

Fuck, I can't hold myself back. I start thrusting faster and faster. Harder and harder.

Gillian's whimpering sounds as she clings to me while I slide in and out of her bare are the most beautiful I've ever heard. I'm overtaken by pure ecstasy.

This is what I want. This girl right here. This woman. *My* woman. Forever...

"I'm coming," she breathes. And when she screams her release, I can't hold mine either.

As we both come down from what happened, I hold her to me. This is where she should belong. Right here, in my arms. However, she can never be mine, not truly.

Tonight was a claiming of sorts. I made her mine, even if she'll never know it and I can never own up to it. But this also needs to be a goodbye, because the way my heart is beating and this feeling is overtaking me, I know this can only mean one thing, and that thing can never be. Not between us.

So, I hold her tighter, kiss her forehead, her eyes, her nose, her mouth. For just this once, I'll allow myself to show her how much she means to me. I'll show her how much I... love her.

I love her. So much.

But I can never tell her. Because feelings are not allowed between us. We are forbidden. And I'm already in too deep.

So, even if she doesn't know it yet, as soon as I get her home, we are saying goodbye forever.

1

———

GILLIAN

PRESENT DAY

I'VE NEVER LIKED HOSPITALS. I CAN NEVER SEEM TO GET comfortable no matter how I cross my legs in these waiting room chairs. Of course it doesn't help that Stella, my daughter, has her head on my lap, waffling in and out of an impromptu nap. I can't blame her. It's been a marathon of a day.

Harley, the second to youngest of the Solace sisters, went into labor early this morning with her first baby.

Everything has happened so fast, from her pregnancy to falling in love, to getting engaged to her now fiancé, Grant Neville. Boy, was that dramatic. But now, we're all happy as clams.

I was her first phone call, if you can believe it. We've come a long way from our past sibling rivalry. But since I'm the only mom of the five of us (until now, that is), she and I formed a close bond as I helped her through her pregnancy.

So, I rallied the troops. Dana, Kira, Amy, Dad, Stella, and me have been here since three A.M. camped out in the waiting room. Doesn't matter that it's her first labor and will probably take all day. This is just the Solace way.

Victoria, supermodel and Grant's younger sister, arrived shortly after we did and cancelled her full day of photo shoots and a red-carpet appearance to be here. "I'm not missing the birth of my first niece for Versace," she explained. Then, my best friend, Lola got here an hour ago after keeping an eye on the bakery we run together. Harley's got a full house waiting for her.

Stella stirs in my lap, stretching out her legs and sighing. I brush her blonde hair, same shade as mine, around the crest of her ear and smile.

"Is the baby here yet, Mommy?" she asks, blinking her eyes open, corners crinkling.

We're the spitting image of one another except those eyes. Mine brown, hers a gorgeous green. Like leaves and bark. Together, we are our own little tree. "Not yet, honey."

"Dad, you're going to create a hole in the floor if you keep pacing," Dana pipes up in her chair across from mine. Dana's the eldest of us and is, consequently, the caretaker, especially since our mom left.

I look across the waiting area at our dad. He's been pacing for the last hour since the doctor let us know Harley was getting ready to push.

Amy pats the chair beside her. "Come sit and relax, Daddy." Amy's the youngest. Always as sweet as a peach... unless she's not, in which case she's a menace.

"Pacing won't make the baby come faster," Kira, the middlest, says in her usually rational, clipped cadence.

"Can't help it, I'm nervous," Dad says, pushing a hand through his hair.

Victoria puts her magazine down on her lap, her lacquered nails clacking against the pages. "You know Grant is taking good care of her, Kent."

Dad grimaces and I can't help but laugh. Grant is Dad's

best friend since their fraternity days. The fact that Grant and Harley somehow found their way into each other's arms still hits him funny on certain occasions.

"Oh, don't make that face," Victoria says, smacking her magazine against his leg.

"You'd think you haven't done this five times before from the way you're acting," Lola says. Lola is practically a sixth Solace sister. After all, she grew up right next door and we've been friends with her since we were in diapers. Lola and I just happened to be in the same grade and managed to be desk mates all through elementary school, so I get her as *my* best friend.

Dad sighs and crosses his arms over his chest. "It's different being out here than in there. At least when you're in there you know what's going on and where you stand. Out here, I have no idea if something is going wrong or..."

"The doctor said she was doing great when she came out, Daddy. Let's just trust the process, huh?" I say with a smile.

He looks over at me, Stella in my lap. The nervousness on his face softens. "Can you believe? Five years ago?"

"Six!" Stella replies with a scolding tone. "I'm six now, grandpa."

Dad clutches his heart. "Six. You're right. They grow up so fast, don't they?"

Yes, they do. Way too fast. Six years ago I was getting ready to be a single mom and terrified of the future. Now, I'm twenty-nine, my daughter's a kindergartener, and life is cruising down the highway.

Dad comes over and reaches for Stella. She latches onto him fast and leaps into his arms.

"Dad, your back!" I cry out. She's average for her age,

not particularly big or small, but she's not as pick uppable as she used to be.

"Oh, relax, I'm fine!" he replies, holding Stella on his hip and rocking her back and forth.

I can't help but smile as she tucks her head on his shoulder. The first Solace grandchild. Sooner than anyone expected, probably. But Dad never flinched away from me with disappointment or concern. He was with me every step of my pregnancy, even held my hand in the delivery room. He was the first person to hold her, after me of course. Because of that, Stella and her grandfather will always have a deep bond. More of a father figure than her father will ever be.

"Gillian–" Lola pokes my arm. She points up at the TV screen in the corner. It's the seven o'clock nightly news; I can tell by the logo in the corner and the ticker rolling by on the bottom of the screen, but that's not really what catches my eye.

It's the image of me helming a protest in front of the empty lot near Stella's school. I'm holding a bullhorn and shaking a sign high in the air that reads, "Community, not condos!" while a crowd with various other signs shouts back at me in solidarity.

"Turn it up, turn it up," Dana says.

Kira rushes to pull a chair out in front of the television and gets up onto it to turn up the volume. As she does, the voice of a newscaster gets clearer.

"...another weekend of protests at the Seton playlot ended with a standoff between protesters and developers."

The footage shifts to a few men in suits approaching the crowd of people. One of the suits is, unfortunately, not just a suit.

It's Lola's brother, Axel Hitchins.

"Oh god," she mutters next to me, tucking her head in her hand as if she can't watch it.

"The protesters, made up of mostly parents from Seton Elementary School, have been trying to stall plans for a new condo building being built by Hitchins Property Developers that will take over the lot that has historically been linked to Seton Elementary. However, the school's lack of ownership over the land and zoning issues keep things at an impasse on both sides."

"You're famous, Gilly," Amy says cheekily.

I'd rather not be. At least not for this. For the past two months, protecting the play lot by Stella's school has taken up all the time I'm not working at the bakery or being a mom. "It wasn't a standoff. All they did was come to survey and we said no," I say as if it's the most pedestrian thing in the world.

Thankfully, they don't show the shouting match Axel and I got into only a few moments later.

Before I can retune into the broadcast, my phone starts ringing in my pocket. I pull it out and find it's Fran Shapiro, my lawyer and fellow parent at Stella's school. Her son, Jacob, and Stella have had many playdates dedicated exclusively to Lego while Fran and I go over the case we have against Hitchins.

"Fran, what's up?" I answer quietly. I can feel Lola shrink further into her chair.

"The temporary hold has gone through. It's going to be brought to city council."

I can't hold back my absolute delight. I gasp, "Are you serious?"

"Serious as I'll ever be. Just got word five minutes ago and called you."

"This is fantastic!"

Fran huffs, "It's *something*. We can't get ahead of ourselves."

"Of course not, but–" I can't find words. I've been a part of protests before. Usually, though, it's just a formality. Just a fucking show of support for something. It's rare anything actually gets done. This time, though, something *might* actually get fixed. We might be able to protect the play lot next to the school. "Thanks for calling to tell me. What's next?"

"Honey, just relax. You've got a baby on the way," Fran chuckles.

Fran and I have become fast friends through this process. She's about fifteen years older than me, but motherhood transcends age. It's amazing how you connect with other moms just based on the fact you're both moms. "Okay, you're right."

"Just celebrate the win and give that baby a big fat kiss for me when you get to. Aw, I want another one."

"Not too late, Fran..."

"Don't even think about it, my husband would kill me. Anyway. Talk soon, Gill."

Fran hangs up before I can reply as is her way. She's a full-time lawyer and a mother with a penchant for scheduling. Every minute she has is worth its weight in gold.

"I wish you'd just drop this, Gillian."

I look at Lola with a raised brow. "Excuse me?"

"It's just–"

"Aren't you proud of me?"

My friend sighs, brushing her dark hair out of her face. "Of course, I am. It's just...you know, I'm sort of between a rock and a hard place with all of this."

"Which is why we don't talk about it," I reply. We

promised to put an embargo on talk about the development as soon as I got involved.

"Gillian, it's been so hard on Axel. He's barely even sleeping because of all this."

My insides twist and my lips pucker like I've just bit into a lemon. I have to hold my tongue or else a torrent of curse words might pour out of me. Since we became adults, Axel is a sore subject. Me and him don't get along for a variety of reasons. I know that the Hitchins company is what Lola's whole family grew up on, their bread and butter. But she's different than them...I wish she wouldn't protect Axel and his feelings so much when he's causing such harm to the community.

I keep this all inside. It wouldn't be helpful to say. Plus, even if I wanted to argue, right now couldn't be a worse time.

We're saved from awkwardness when Harley's doctor walks in with a serene smile on her face. All of us are silent, but Dad manages to croak out, "What's the word, doc?"

The doctor's smile grows. "Why don't you come back and see for yourself?"

***

"Be very careful, Stella. Support her head..." I say softly, crouching next to my daughter who is sitting in a chair at Harley's bedside. In her arms is little Tana Neville, Harley's daughter. Fresh out of the womb and red-faced.

Tana already met her grandfather, auntie, and all her aunts. Now it's Stella's turn. She was miraculously patient, though she ran from person to person, eagerly looking up at them to try and get another glimpse of the baby.

Harley looks on from her bed, eyes lazing tiredly, and

her short hair frizzed from sweat. The smile on her face, though, hasn't disappeared for one second. The work she just did is no joke. I should know.

"What do I say?" Stella asks, looking to Harley and then to me.

"Introduce yourself," Dad says from behind the chair, looking down as his two grandchildren meet for the first time.

"Hi Tana," Stella says. "I'm Stella. I'm your cousin. I was the first one here, so you need to respect me."

"Stella," I admonish.

"Don't worry, she will," Harley says with a gentle laugh.

"Needs to learn to respect those who came before her," Grant adds with a deferential nod toward Stella.

Harley and Grant exchange a look of love that's so intense every one of us can feel it. I hate to say I'm jealous, but I am. Harley deserves it. Each and every one of my sisters does. And yet, love like that seems to elude me. Especially now that I'm a mother. Who has the time?

Before Stella, for a while, I had a boyfriend, love, I had found someone. I had looked for my person and was determined to have my happy ever after, my mother's abandonment be damned. I saw how she and Dad were before everything fell apart. It felt real. Some of that *must* have been real. So, I searched high and low for that, determined that, unlike my mother, I wouldn't screw up my family. I would run headfirst into love at any cost and I had found the perfect guy.

Unfortunately for past me, it didn't last forever. When we were done, it hurt.

When the perfect chance for a rebound happened, I was all in. Stupidly, in time I fell for him, but he didn't feel the same. We ended things.

So, you could say I was a bit surprised to learn about my unplanned pregnancy. More than a bit, actually. I thought I'd been careful. I'd been wrong.

"She's *big*," Stella mutters with wide eyes.

"You're telling me," Harley grumbles.

I laugh. "You're in good spirits."

"Oh, of course, how could I not be?" she replies.

I go to her bedside and plant a kiss on her forehead. "You did so good, sissy."

Harley sighs in relief. "Thanks, Gilly."

I look at Grant. "How are *you* holding up?"

His blue eyes widen. "Good. Better than I...expected."

"I only cursed him out a couple times."

"Like I said, better than expected." Grant chuckles. Then, he looks down at Harley. "I'm very lucky."

Another pang to my heart. *You're happy for them, Gillian. Stay happy.* "And don't you forget it," I say, wagging my finger at him playfully.

"I won't. Promise."

I swallow and nod. "Good." I need a break from all the lovey-dovey, so I turn back to my daughter. She's in good hands with Dad behind her and Dana now crouching where I once was. On the other side of the room, Kira, Victoria, and Amy are arranging a food order for Harley. She's desperate for sushi since she wasn't able to eat it while pregnant.

I'll leave them to that and instead go to the window where Lola is leaning, taking in the whole scene. "Thanks for inviting me, Gill," she murmurs.

"Of course. You're family, Lola," I reply. It's true to me beyond a shadow of a doubt.

She smiles at me and holds up her pinky finger. I put my pinky up to hers and we squeeze them together. An unspoken tradition between us, something we've done over and over since we were little. The love is always there regardless of what happens between us. I hope. "You know…" she says with a sigh, looking back at Harley and Grant as Dad helps return the baby into Harley's arms. "I'm glad we have a pact about Axel being off-limits."

I do a double take. "Wha-what?! Why are you bringing *that* up?" It's been a rule since we hit puberty. Axel was off limits to me; my sisters were off limits to her (on the off chance her sexuality took a turn toward the female persuasion).

"Just cause…" Lola jerks her head subtly toward Grant and Harley. "The drama, ya know?"

I glance back at my family. Yeah, there was a lot of drama. There was a lot of arguing, at least one punch involved, and some work to get us all to a point where our sort-of-uncle Grant was now more than that. "But it all worked out. They're happy. It doesn't matter how they got there, it's just…" I trail off as I look at Lola. "Never mind. Yeah. You're right."

What Lola doesn't know can't hurt her.

2

AXEL

"Do you know what this is going to cost me?"

I blink at my father. Best to stay quiet when he's angry to keep his blood pressure down.

"*Axel.*"

Unless he demands a response. Then it's best to actually *respond.* "A lot of money."

"Yeah. A *lot of fucking money,*" Dad growls and throws the newspaper down on his desk. "I should have known twenty years ago that she was going to be a troublemaker." On the very front page is a picture of Gillian with her bullhorn and "Community, not condos!" sign overhead, looking as vicious as a wild beast. He's somehow managed to get the issue before it went to print. Just the Hitchins way. Throwing money at the problem to get what he wants. Or someone owed him a favor.

I straighten up. I haven't bothered to sit down. That way I can always make a quick getaway if he loses his temper. "I'll take care of it," I say, as if there won't be any problem. However, knowing Gillian, there will *definitely* be a problem. I just have to give my dad some sort of confidence so I can get out of here unscathed.

"Oh, will you?" Dad asks sarcastically.

"It's not a problem." On the outside, I remain calm even though, inside, I'm screaming at myself. "Taking care" of anything when it comes to Gillian Solace is *definitely* a problem. However, I'll spin whatever tale I need to make sure Dad stays happy. Otherwise, he might cast me aside just like he did Jeremiah, my older brother. Unlike Jeremiah, I'm not more passionate about my social causes than our family name and legacy. Not to mention the money. Yeah, it's mostly about the money.

"Axel, if you could have handled this problem, then we would have had this nipped in the bud yesterday. In fact, there never would have been a protest and we would have already broken ground," Dad grumbles, leaning back in his seat. Even in his home office, he's every bit the businessman he is when we're at the Hitchins Property Development headquarters. "So, forgive me for not having a lot of faith that you're going to be able to handle this without me throwing a couple bribes over to the city council."

If Jeremiah could see us now, he'd be losing his lunch. He's working somewhere in Africa building schools and wells for remote villages. Good for him, I guess. Couldn't be me. "Like I said, I'll get Gillian to back off, alright? Lola is already—"

"*Don't* get me started on Lola," Dad spits, pulling out a handkerchief and dabbing his forehead. Now a septuagenarian, the man's health is starting to worry me. "No, Gillian Solace is far too hard-headed for Lola to break down. They're too close." Dad eyes me, green meeting green. "You'll do it. You don't care about Gillian Solace's feelings, do you?"

I gulp. "Nope."

"Great. It's business, right?"

I glance out the window of Dad's office. It has a view of the second floor of the Solace home. Back in the day, things seemed so simple. Gillian was just my kid sister's best friend. Now she's actively plotting my demise.

Stiff upper lip, Axel. You don't need friends. You need this project to go through.

This was supposed to be my first major build to kick off Dad's retirement plan. Of course, with Dad, he's scheduled his retirement into phases that will last five years. The man's swimming in money but will be a workaholic until the day he dies, that is very clear.

That plan is completely up in the air now that Gillian has helmed with protest and practical smear campaign against Hitchins Property Development, preventing us from making any moves on getting this condo built.

It's been nothing but a pain my ass.

But how the hell do I deal with Gillian?

Your guess is as good as mine.

"Just, you know, give her options. I'm happy to throw some money her way so she can send that kid of hers to a private school instead of Seton. Although Kent should have the money, shouldn't he?"

I roll my eyes. "You know her. She's into all of that stuff." Since we were little, Gillian has been very righteous. Miss Holier-Than-Thou with her veganism and her emphasis on community care. Always thinking she's better than everyone though she's just mucking about. The sad thing is nothing will ever change.

That's why I try not to get involved. Keep things simple. I work, I play, I have my morning runs and that's that. Nothing complicated. No *causes*. No passion.

Maybe something is wrong with me, but I'm okay with that. Passion just makes life complicated.

I've learned that the hard way.

"Right...community, not condos," Dad says and then pretends to gag.

My phone buzzes in my pocket. I whip it out and see a text from Lola.

Come meet Harley's baby!

I sigh. I told her I'd come. I'm not a monster. After all, the Solace girls and us Hitchins have been friends since childhood. Just because we've grown in different directions doesn't mean that shared history just disappears. "Dad, I gotta go. Harley just had her baby and–"

"Yes, go, go. I have to start making some calls."

I give him a sympathetic glance. "Will you please get to bed on time tonight?"

My father's bulldoggish expression softens. "Axel–"

"Your doctor says you need your eight hours."

He sighs. "Yes, I'll go to sleep on time."

He's such a bad liar. "And your meds. Don't forget to take–"

"I'll be fine. Go, son."

I look at my dad one last moment before leaving. I feel like there's a lock at the base of my neck, pulling all my bones too close together. Hopefully, I can get in and out of this without going toe to toe with Gillian.

Otherwise, we might have a problem.

I PRESS the glowing elevator button for the fifteenth time. This elevator is so fucking slow. I've been standing here waiting for it for what feels like ages. In reality, it probably hasn't been more than thirty seconds. I don't know why I'm in so much of a rush. Not like this baby is going to get up and leave. But I'm always in a rush these days. Always trying to get things done as fast as possible. Some might say I have a problem with work-life balance, but that's not a problem when your work *is* your life.

The elevator finally dings, a red light glowing above the one that's arrived.

"Finally," I mumble to myself and walk right up to the silver doors to sneak through as fast as possible.

I've made a terrible calculation, though, and forgotten to leave berth for anyone coming off the elevator. As soon as they slide open, I feel my face go paper white.

"Yes, we can go, but stop jumping so we can–" Gillian Solace comes off the elevator with her head turned back, eyes on her daughter, Stella, and walks smack into me before I can step aside. "Oh my god!" she exclaims, her face snapping to mine with terror in her eyes.

I get a flash of the image of her I just saw in the paper, her passionate fury almost slapping me in the face. "Sorry, sorry, I–"

"Axel, what the–" she stops short of cursing and clutches the neckline of her floral peasant blouse. "What are you doing here?"

I start to respond, but Gillian quickly snaps her attention back to her daughter. "Come on, come on! Before the doors close."

Stella leaps off the elevator, taking Gillian's hand.

"I'm here to see Harley." I push down every thought I've had about her on the way over here, all the ways I can try and worm my way into her head and make her back off. This just...isn't the time.

Gillian shakes her head as if she's somehow forgotten that's where *she's* just come from. "Right. Of course. That's nice of you." She emphasizes nice as if I've never been nice in my life.

"Yeah, well," I reply, watching the doors close behind her. Yes, I hurry in every aspect of my life. But when it comes to Gillian, I... don't. Besides, walking away would probably be a death sentence. She'd most likely shout after me that I was scared to face her or something. And that's not the case. Not at all.

Okay, that'd be a lie.

I've been scared of her my whole life but *extra* scared for the past seven years since–

"We were just talking about you!" Stella peeps, jumping up on her tiptoes.

I look down at her and smile. Stella has always been a particularly outgoing little girl. So much like Gillian that being friends with her almost feels like Gillian and I are still friends somehow.

Almost. Because no one could really replace Gillian.

"Oh yeah? Good things I hope?" I speak.

Stella looks up at her mother with wide eyes. "Um..."

Okay, bad things. I'm sure Stella has gotten a whole earful from her mother about the Seton play lot. I wonder if she sees me as an enemy.

For now, though, with her tender ears right nearby, we'll be on our best behavior.

Maybe not best, just behavior.

"You know what?" Gillian interrupts, holding up a hand and forcing a smile. "Stella, if you want that ice cream, we're going to have to go now before it's too late. I don't want you up past your bedtime and it's already–" Gillian reaches into the pocket of her tight khakis for her phone, but struggles.

"Eight-ten," I answer for her.

"I can do it," she mumbles under her breath, pulling out her phone and reading the time aloud. "Eight-ten."

"Wow, that late already?" I say dryly.

Gillian glares at me, brown eyes scalding. "Anyway, we should be–"

Suddenly, Stella touches my hand. "Do you want ice cream, Axel?"

I resist jerking my hand away like she's some sort of diseased leper. It's not that I don't like kids. I just can't imagine Gillian wants her daughter touching me.

Before I can respond, Gillian tugs Stella away. "Axel is here to see Aunt Harley and the new baby, sweetheart. Maybe–" Gillian eyes me again. "Maybe another time."

Code for 'How about never?'

"Say buh-bye, honey," Gillian says, starting off toward the door with Stella.

Stella looks over her shoulder at me, her big green eyes looking puppyish and sad. Not sure why she wants to spend time with an old guy like me, but...it is flattering that a little kid might think I'm cool enough to hang out with.

Then, my eyes travel to a place I try and stay away from. Gillian's ass. God, she filled out so nicely after her pregnancy. She was always beautiful and curvy, but something about becoming a mom just did something to her figure. I feel ashamed even thinking about it.

But I know how she felt before. The width of her hips, the creaminess of her thighs, the heavenly scent of her neck.

What does she feel like now?

"Wait!" I call out. *What the fuck are you doing, dude?*

Stella flips around first, smile reappearing on her lips followed by Gillian who is much less smiley.

Still. I can't help it. Gillian has always intoxicated me. I've kept her at arm's length for years now after we crossed a line while Lola was away doing volunteer work. I've never been able to forget that summer as much as I've tried to push her away and tune out her noise.

Gillian Solace is just too much for me to ignore. Now that we are locked in this standoff, I'm in her thrall all over again. Sure, she's a pain in my ass.

But what was it Sun Tzu said? Know thy enemy or something?

Sure. That's what I'm trying to do. Get to know my enemy.

"You have something to say?" Gillian asks in my silence.

"Y-yes! Yes, um." I stride over to them, trying to maintain an affable smile. "Look, I don't think Harley probably wants a visitor like me this late in the day. I'll come by tomorrow. Let me join you guys."

Now it's Gillian's turn to pale. "Axel, I–"

"Yippee!" Stella cries out, jumping up and down. "Ice cream party!"

Gillian's brow locks together; she looks down at Stella and sighs. I know she can't deny Stella her happiness. Not when she's such a sweet, cute kid.

"It'll be fun," I say firmly and reach into my pocket for my car key. "I'll drive."

Gillian chews on the corner of her lower lip, shakes her head, and then sighs. "Fine. But no speeding."

"I can manage that," I reply. This might be a bad idea. But I can't help it. Anger and desire are so close to one another that I must be getting confused. *Stick to the plan. Play nice, get some intel. Get this shit built.*

"We'll see about that." Is that...is that a smirk on her lips?

With that, Gillian walks with Stella out the front door of the hospital, expecting me to follow.

I need a moment alone, though. She'll castrate me if she's seen I've gotten hard just by talking to her.

3

GILLIAN

I stare at the many flavors in the ice cream counter. There are two vegan options, and of course, a couple sorbets, so that's where I'll go if I decide the calories are worth it. In the meantime, Stella is bouncing up and down the length of the counter, unable to decide what sounds best to her.

"Cookie dough? Or birthday cake?" Stella wonders aloud.

"I'm partial to buttered pecan myself," Axel says with a smile.

"Just like grandpa!" Stella says with a smile gape as if Axel and her grandfather sharing a favorite ice cream is the most novel thing in the world.

Axel grimaces. "Well, when you put it like that..."

I can't help but laugh to myself. *Yes, my dear, keep him humbled.* "Is that what you're getting?" I ask.

"I was going to until I was called old by your daughter."

Ouch. That stings. *Your.* Like I somehow manifested her in my womb without help.

"I'm surprised you let her have ice cream."

I frown at him.

"Cause milk, ya know?"

I sigh. "Raising a kid vegan is very difficult. I couldn't handle that on top of everything else required of being a single mother." That's my jab back even if he might not feel it as harshly as I'd like him to.

"Of course," he says carefully. "I just thought since you're so *passionate* about your *causes*–"

I turn to him, ire flaming in all of my nerves. "Are you really doing this here?" I hiss.

Axel smiles. *Damn him.* He's got a gorgeous smile. I noticed it when I was twelve. It was smart of Lola to make a rule that I could never date her brother because I was hooked on him from the moment I started experiencing "the changes" (as Mom put it).

"Relax, she's not paying attention."

I glance back at Stella. She's managed to ask the woman working behind the counter for a sample of something bright orange. Hopefully, the sugar makes her crash rather than bouncing off the walls all night. "Is this why you invited yourself along for ice cream with me and my daughter? To corner me and–"

"Whoa, whoa, whoa," Axel stops me, holding up his hands. I suck in a breath at the size of his palms, remembering the feeling of them all over me. *Gillian. No.* "Who said anything about cornering you? I'd never do *that*."

I narrow my eyes. "Right."

"You know, this whole feud between the two of us is ridiculous, don't you think?"

He's talking about his property development, but my mind goes back years and years. This feud has been going on a lot longer. In fact, it started back in our teen years when he started picking on me and I realized it was flirting.

I couldn't do anything about it because of my promise to Lola, so I picked on him right back. It was only a matter of time before the dynamite went off. And while dynamite might be explosive, it leaves only destruction in its wake.

"Let's put an end to it, huh? I know it's been hard on both of us. And Lola too, so—"

"How do you suppose we 'put an end to it', Axel?" I ask, leaning on the counter with an expectant look on my face.

Axel sighs. "You know I'm not backing off, Gillian."

"Great. Well, this conversation hasn't been very productive, has it?" I say and turn back toward Stella on my heels. "Do you know what you want, sweetie?"

"I still can't decide between birthday cake and cookie dough," Stella sighs.

"And why should you?" Axel says. He pushes past me and gestures toward the woman behind the counter. "A double scoop for the little lady, huh?"

"Axel!" I cry out.

He ignores me, touching Stella on the shoulder. My entire body braces and I go mute. No energy to fight him even though I know that two scoops is far too much for my little girl. It's just...the image of them together twists my heart so tight it feels like it might combust.

"What is it you wanted, sweetheart?" he asks Stella.

"Birthday cake and cookie dough. In a waffle cone."

"You heard the woman," he says with a nod. Then, he looks over at me. "What are you having, Gillian?"

My lips tighten. "A scoop of the coconut sorbet. In a cup please."

Axel rolls his eyes. "'In a cup'. You don't know how to have fun anymore, do you, Gillian?"

Anymore. Like he remembers all the fun we had together throughout the years. Running around in the sprinkler as kids, getting ready for school dances as teens, the tremendous ease of our bodies looping around one another in young adulthood.

Maybe I was too reckless. Young and accidentally pregnant.

I wouldn't trade Stella for the world. For the *whole* world.

But I had to grow up very fast to make sure I was ready for her. Every day, I'm still growing up even though I'm twenty-nine. I have to be my best self for her.

So, when Axel says I don't know how to have *fun* anymore...well, that just makes me want to incinerate him even more.

We get our ice creams and go sit at a parlor table. I barely touch my sorbet while I watch Stella lap at her double scoop. Axel quietly licks a scoop of butter pecan. I fume the longer we sit there until I think I might burst.

"Stella, honey–" I reach into my purse and pull out a couple of quarters. "Go pick out some songs on the jukebox, would you?" The place is as old-fashioned as can be with all the same fixtures it must have had back in the fifties, jukebox included.

"She's not finished with her ice cream," Axel says, aware I'm trying to send her away so I can give him a piece of my mind.

"She can multitask," I say dryly as I place the coins in my daughter's hand.

She leaps up and then curtseys. "Any requests?"

I can't help but giggle the tiniest bit. She's got ice cream across her chin and lips like it's lipstick and a huge splotch of it on the front of her shirt. Kids will be kids. "Whatever you like, Stella."

"If they've got anything by the Rat Pack–" Axel pauses.

"You know the Rat Pack, kiddo?"

Kiddo.

Stella snorts. "Of course I know the *Rat Pack.*"

"Of course she knows the Rat Pack," Axel flashes a smile my way which makes me melt against my wishes. "Okay, make it count, then."

Stella skips off, her ice cream cone tenuously balanced in her hand.

"She's really darling, Gillian," Axel says, watching as she goes off.

That's about enough from you, Axel. I slam my hand down on the table. "Listen, Axel, and listen to me carefully."

His eyebrows raise in alarm, green eyes snapping to me.

"I'm not backing down until the city council gives their verdict. And even then, I won't back down."

Axel is quiet for a moment. Then, he smiles lopsidedly. *Jackass.* "You're so passionate, Gillian."

"Don't say that like I'm a kid, Axel. I might be younger than you, but I'm not a kid." I look off in Stella's direction. "Not anymore."

"It's just an empty lot, Gillian."

"It's not!" I say, trying to keep my voice low, though my emotions are red hot. "The kids who go to Seton have been playing in that lot since the nineteen fifties. It's a community tradition."

He tsks and tosses his hand in my direction as if trying to disperse me like I'm a bunch of marbles. "Gillian, Seton doesn't *own* the lot. It never has. You know there are protocols and laws in place for things like this. And *we* own the property."

"It's not property! It's land, it's earth, it's–"

"You know that hippie shit doesn't work on me."

My mouth tightens. Who does he think he is, speaking to me like that?

"I appreciate it, Gillian, I...really do, but business is business. And you're making my work a lot harder for me than–" Axel stops suddenly and looks in the direction of the jukebox as a song starts to waft through the air.

A song we both know too well.

"Those fingers in my hair...that sly come-hither stare..."

"How about that, huh?" Axel says and then tries to laugh, eyes cast down on the table.

"That strips my conscience bare, it's witchcraft..."

I shake my head. "She likes that song a lot. I had nothing to do with it."

This is the most either of us have said in reference to our connection all those summers ago. A song that played that very first time. 'Witchcraft' by Frank Sinatra. I never forgot it.

I guess Axel hasn't either.

Axel clears his throat. "Anyway. Back to business–"

"No," I say firmly. "No more business. I'm done talking about it, Axel."

His forehead pinches in the center.

"I'm done," I repeat. "You know my position and I know yours."

"You're making this so hard on yourself, Gillian."

I shake my head. "No, I'm making it hard on *you*. That's what you don't like. And, Axel, there is nothing I like more than making your life difficult."

We stare at each other, the song that means so much to our pathetic story playing in the background.

Axel sucks on his lower lip and nods. "Alright. Point taken."

It better be.

4

AXEL

THE REST OF THE VISIT TO THE ICE CREAM PARLOR IS
tense. Thank god Stella is there to make things a little
easier. She's none the wiser to the awkwardness between
her mother and myself. She manages to lead us in a bright,
bubbling conversation about music. She's a charismatic little
girl who loves roller-skates and struggles with math (her
words, not mine).

Once she's managed to get down more of her ice
cream cone than a girl her size should be able to, we
decide to call it a night, or should I say, *Gillian* decides to
call it a night.

I can feel the regret pouring off of her as we walk back
to my car. *Why did I offer to drive and extend this misery?*

I don't know what I was thinking trying to convince her
to back down from her protests. Gillian Solace never backs
down from anything. I should know.

"What's your address?" I ask in a small voice after we
pile into the car.

Gillian holds her hand out for my phone without saying
anything. I give it to her; she types in the address quickly

before handing it back to me. Her eyes are staring squarely straight ahead.

"Jeez, tough crowd," I say with a little wry humor.

The car is silent.

"Okay, let's go."

Gillian lives in Silver Lake, close to the bakery she and Lola run. I've been trying to get them a space in Hollywood for a second location. I'm very tempted to stop my search on that because of Gillian's attitude, but Lola is my sister. I'll do it for her, even if I'm gritting my teeth the whole time.

"Can you turn on the radio?" Stella asks from the backseat.

I eye her in the rearview mirror as we get on the highway and smile. "Sure, kiddo."

I hear Gillian huff in the seat beside me. Didn't know "kiddo" was so inflammatory to her. I turn on the radio, static settling out into a rock song I can't identify because my brain is filled with swarming thoughts.

I get it. I ambushed her. But it's the only way I can get a word in with her these days. Lola has made the bakery strictly off-limits for any sort of business talk because of the time Gillian and I were mid-argument in the kitchen and she burst a piping bag full of frosting all over the place due to her temper.

If her anger wasn't directed at me, I'd say it was sexy. Otherwise, it's just terrifying.

We continue down the highway until the appropriate exit and, as I turn onto the residential streets, I glance into the rearview again to look at Stella.

She's slouched over against the window, mouth lolled open with sleep. Gosh, what a cutie. I can never stay mad at Gillian for too long when I remember how sweet her little girl is. Gillian might hate my guts (perhaps deservedly...), but she's doing something right with her daughter, that's for sure.

I feel a pang in my chest. I'm thirty-two. No prospects. And no intention of settling down or finding a woman. I've felt that way for years now.

Sometimes, though, in moments like this...well, I can't help but think about fatherhood. Wouldn't it be nice to have a little part of me running around, combined with a part of someone else I hopefully loved with all my heart and soul?

Parenting is hard work. The hardest job I can fathom. I don't want to negate that. However, the older I've gotten and the more people I know having had babies, the more worthwhile it seems.

"The yellow door on the left," Gillian says softly, pointing out the window.

I look out at the house she's pointing at. It's lit up in the night with a few lights lining the walkway and a porch light that indeed shows off a yellow door under a white portico.

"Thanks for the ride," Gillian goes on. Feels like she's pulling her own teeth to say it.

"No problem. Always happy to get you home safe." And it's the truth.

She puts her hand on the door handle.

Something propels me out of the car at lightning speed. I'm not done with this yet. I'm not just going to let Gillian go inside and leave things this way. I might not be able to fix things in the blink of an eye, but I don't want her to think I'm just a monster. We grew up together, for God's sake.

Doesn't she have *any* positive memories of me?

"I got her," I say.

"Axel, really, you don't–"

I ignore her and throw open Stella's door. The little girl rubs her eyes and blinks up at me. "Home?"

"Yes, honey. Let's get you in bed, okay?" I unclip her seatbelt and pick Stella up in my arms. She holds onto me without hesitation. I must make her feel safe. I hope I do.

Gillian appears at my elbow. "Axel, I can take her inside, really."

"I've already got her," I murmur. Stella buries her head in my neck and sighs. "You go open the door, alright?"

Gillian's hard exterior melts for just a moment. She nods before leading me up the walk toward the yellow door. I take each step with the utmost care, making sure to watch my footing and not to jostle Stella too much as she's already fallen asleep on my shoulder.

Gillian opens the door and holds it open for me. "Her room is at the end of the hallway. Her name is on the door."

I step into Gillian's little Silver Lake bungalow. The main room is a living room that leads directly into the kitchen. Even in the dark, I can see it embodies Gillian to a tee. Macrame accents, Moroccan rugs, rattan furniture. All tied together with the mess of having a kid around. There are toys and shoes littering the floor, a sink full of dishes, and the distinct smell of playdoh wafts through the air. It feels loved and lived-in. A true home.

I carry Stella down the short hallway, passing two doors that I imagine are the bathroom and Gillian's room. Both closed. I'd love a glimpse at what her bedroom looks like. If it's anything like the Gillian I used to know, there's probably a mountain of unfolded clothes and candles half burnt littering the room.

Indeed, Stella's room is marked with a personalized name plaque, the kind parents get when their babies are first born. Her name is scrawled in baby blue, accented with stars. Stella. Gillian's little star.

I open the door, wincing when it squeals open. Stella doesn't stir, though.

Gillian hurries in after me. "Here—" She goes to the little twin bed against the opposite wall and pulls down the comforter.

I lean down and lay Stella down in the bed. Her arms sink down to her side and she curls into her pillow with a satisfied sigh. I have to say, I miss the little girl in my arms, her heart beating against my chest. Having something to protect is a nice feeling. Better than fighting for the development of a luxury condo, that's for sure.

I pull the blanket up over Stella softly and run my hand down her arm without thinking. That's when I feel Gillian's stare from across the bed. I look up, expecting laser eyes, but instead...well, I can't quite read her look. It's just intense. That's the only way I can put it.

She looks away. "Um..."

"I'll...leave you to say goodnight."

I back out of the room and go back to the living room, unsure if I should stay or go. Before I can make a decisions, Gillian's voice comes from behind me. "Thank you."

I glance back at her and clutch my heart. "Are you really thanking me? The corporate tyrant?"

"Axel...I'm being serious," she sighs.

I nod. "I know. But there's no thanks needed."

"No, the ice cream and the ride back and carrying her inside...it's a lot easier to have another pair of hands. So, really, thank you."

I bet it's been tough having to go at it alone. Even though her family is as close as can be, I can't imagine it's easy. "Well, you could consider thanking me by not making my life a living nightmare?"

The softness on her face immediately dissipates. Shit. I

really stepped in it, didn't I? Me and my mouth. "Are you being serious right now? I'm trying to be nice, and you want to—"

"I was *just* making a joke."

"It's always jokes with you, Axel! A joke here, a joke there, and yet underneath is the insidious—"

"Oh god, here we go. Let me dust off your soapbox for you," I say quietly, crouching down and pretending to dust off an imaginary platform for her to climb up on and spew her nonsense.

Gillian's hands clench. "You—" She stops, looking over her shoulder, making sure her voice can't be heard down the hall. Then, she takes a few steps toward me. "You will never take me seriously, will you?"

"I never said that."

"You don't have to. Men like you, it's obvious in every word."

I might act like a corporate robot, but I still feel the sting of her words. "Men like me?"

"Yes! All you care about is the bottom line. You don't care about—"

"'Community Care'?" I ask mockingly, air quoting. "Look, Gillian, your buzzwords are losing gravity." Not that they ever had it.

Gillian huffs. "I'm not just buzzwords. Did you know that every day, we lose six thousand acres of open land to people like you building condos that will sit empty for years? There are over ninety thousand units in LA sitting empty while under forty thousand people are unhoused. Think about that!"

I swallow. "It doesn't work like that, and you know it."

"I don't care if it *doesn't* work like that. It *should* work like that. And I'm *fighting* for it to work like that. Trying to show my daughter that our voices matter and that we can make change when people like–" Her eyes focus in on me. Another step toward me. Closer. Somehow closer than ever even though we're still a foot apart. "Do you even care about anything other than making money, Axel?"

"Lots of things."

"Really? That's news to me."

I will not stand here and let her berate me anymore. I am still a human being even if my goals to her are sort of demonic. I step toward her, one more little half step so I'm looking down into her brown eyes, challenging her. "Gillian, you don't get anything by being good or nice or even believing in the right things. You know this. I'm not willing to suffer just to do the right thing. I'm genuinely sorry that my work is at your expense, really, but the things *I* care about are in direct opposition to what you care about. You've made it clear that the measure of a good human is being unwilling to sacrifice or bend for the things you want. Why should I do that for you, then?"

Gillian's upper lip curls up in contempt and then she grits her teeth. "God, I hate you."

Then, without warning, she grabs both sides of my face and kisses me harshly. I have no willpower to resist her, not when all the memories come flooding back.

She pulls away and then repeats right into my mouth. "I hate you so much."

"Oh, yeah?" I wrap my arms around her waist, hands splayed out against her lower back and pull her hips flush to mine. "Then show me, Gillian. Show me how much you *hate* me."

5

———————

GILLIAN

WHY DID HE HAVE TO WALK INTO MY HOME IN THE dark of night, looking so goddamn sexy as he took care of my daughter and put her to bed? Why despite every piece of me despising him and everything he stands for does my body light up at the idea of him touching me?

Why do I want Axel Hitchins so bad?

Hatefuck is a term I've always abhorred. I've never experienced the propulsion to throw myself at someone because I despised them so much.

Except with this man, because here I am, with my arms around Axel in my living room, desperate to fuck the shit out of him.

His hands slink down from my lower back, grabbing a handful of my ass. His head tilts back, teeth bared, veins protruding in his neck. "Goddammit."

I'm not wasting time trying to contemplate what's happening. I kiss him again harshly and let him catch up to me.

Axel's tongue coaxes my lips open until I feel like he

might devour me. Suddenly, he forces me back harshly against the wall. I gasp and almost melt into his arms.

"Why do you have to stand there and piss me off, Gillian?" Axel whispers tensely and then presses a line of kisses up my neck until his lips reach my ear. "Why can't you just back off and–

"You know I don't back down from a challenge."

Is that a smile on his lips? "Yeah, I know."

I shake my head. "You're not getting off so easily."

"Fine."

"Fine."

I let every care fade away–my daughter in the next room, my best friend who has made Axel repeatedly off-limits to me, the fact it's been years since someone's been inside me–and I go for what I want.

I reach down between us and grab for his cock. He's already hard through his pants.

"Jesus Christ," he mutters, shock and pleasure from my touch colliding.

I wrap my other hand around the back of his head. My fingers thread through his dark hair. "I did this."

"Well, you did promise you'd make things hard for me."

I can't help but laugh. "I said difficult, not hard."

Axel lifts his chin. Eyelids lazing low. Glimmering green. Temptation. "Whatever, Gillian. You got your wish."

Was this my wish? From the second I saw Axel in the hospital, my stomach filled with so much dread I felt nauseous. And yet every moment since then, the tension has built and built, embers growing into a blazing fire.

And now, here we are.

Axel grabs my wrists and presses them up to the wall behind me. *"Don't look so fucking smug."*

"Oooh, tough guy," I tease, swaying my hips side to side

against his so that I can feel his hardness through my jeans. God, I missed this.

He grabs both my wrists in one hand as the other slides into the top of my jeans without warning. I don't even have time to react before his fingers curl in between my folds. I gasp, rising on my toes as if I can somehow escape the pleasure I so desperately want. "You're not the only one who can tease, Gillian." His fingers hook inside me.

My mouth falls ajar. I can't stand the man, but his touch has me melting. I don't know if I'm ready to feel good like that. It's been so long. "We can't wake up Stella."

"Should have thought about that before you kissed me." Axel removes his hand from me. I'm embarrassed that I miss his touch immediately. Then, he undoes the closure on my jeans and rips them down to my knees.

"Now you," I whisper.

For a second, his eyes lock with mine and the anger dissipates on his lips. He swallows as if he's about to tell me a secret before undoing his own pants. I stop him halfway through and grab onto the waistband of his slacks. Our eyes harden in each other's before I work his pants down his hips, my fingers grazing the sides of his ass, until his cock bounds free.

"There he is..." I say and then wrap a hand around his shaft.

Axel grunts, both in frustration and arousal and then pushes me up against the wall again, nose nudging against my jaw. "I'm going to fuck you right here."

"No, you're not."

His hands slide down to my bare ass, sending electricity through my body as he slams our hips together. I can feel him hard right at my groin, so close he could slip inside me. "You sure about that?"

I go slack in his arms for a mere moment. Let him think he has control. "Yeah," I say, before pushing him against his shoulders.

Axel stumbles back, catching himself on an armchair. I follow, stepping out of my jeans and then straddling him, trapping him in the chair. He laughs. I know he loves this. Loves the game.

And so do I.

I grab his cock, positioning it against my entrance, and then sink down onto it. Raw, wet, warm.

Perfect.

Axel's body goes rigid with shock. "God fucking dammit, Gillian."

It's been a while, but the stretch...my god, the stretch feels incredible. My head falls back as I let out a long sigh.

Axel, however, does not have patience. He hooks his hands around my hips and drives his cock fully into me. I'm not ready and cry out louder than I intend. I bury my face in the back of the chair, as if I can hide from the sound I made. He chuckles and then says in a low voice, "You weren't ready for me, were you?"

On the contrary, I was absolutely ready for him. So ready. I want us to destroy each other. We've been keeping up this battle of the minds for two months now. It's time for a different kind of combat.

"You fucking drive me crazy, Gillian," Axel grunts, creating a steady tempo with his hips as he drives up into me. I know he doesn't mean it in the good, romantic way. I also know the feeling is mutual. But right now, he is driving me crazy with lust. With want.

I move a hand like a claw up through his hair, digging my nails into the back of his skull, holding on for dear life.

"Tell me how you feel," he whispers.

For a second, I forget we're adversaries and I whisper, "So good."

"Good." He peppers kisses to my collarbone. "That's how I want you to feel."

I drop my hips down onto him, swallowing up his length. Searing pleasure floods through me, made even better by the choking sound he makes. I start to rut my hips against him.

Axel doesn't reply. How could he when he's straining so hard to contain himself from making a sound?

I smile. I needed this so bad. I needed to get laid *so bad*. The past six years have been nothing but work, worry, tension. Lots of joy and excitement, but where does a mother fit into her own life when she's dedicating it to her child?

"You're enjoying this," Axel whispers.

"Is that obvious?"

"I thought you hated me."

"Oh, I do."

Axel grabs my shoulder and rips my sleeve down my arm, releasing one of my breasts from my shirt. He throws himself into my chest and wraps his lips around one of my nipples. That sends a shockwave through me. My steady rhythm of thrusting starts to stutter and jolt at the new feeling.

"Mmmm..." Axel hums against my chest, eyes peeling up toward me. He looks so satisfied.

I take a deep breath, muster my last bit of strength and then...

I go wild.

I hold tight to the back of the chair and buck my hips as hard as I can. I'm going to have him begging for mercy by the time this is over.

Axel's mouth pops off my breast. "How are you going so fast?"

"I need it, Axel, I need it."

"Tell me what you need, baby, tell me." *Baby*. The word shivers up my spine. I grab a handful of his hair and tilt his head back so he can look up into my eyes.

"Need you to make me come."

"I thought you hated me."

I don't. No, I *do*. I hate what he's become. The heartless businessman. The person who will walk on the backs of others to get what he wants, like his father.

That's not the Axel I know he could be.

I bite on my lower lip, rolling my hips tenaciously. He looks as beautiful as a Renaissance painting. His expression is like someone looking up to the heavens praying for some sort of sign. Lips blushed and parted. Eyes plangent and strained. He is the past and the present blending into one right here and my body is reacting to that.

I feel his hands press into my ass so hard he might leave imprints.

"Gillian..." he whispers.

And that utterance of my name...the way he looks so desperate and tender and beautiful...the swelter of dark around us drives my pleasure higher and higher until. "Oh my god, I'm–I'm–" I press my chin to my chest and close my eyes tight. *Don't make a sound. Don't make one fucking sound.*

The orgasm is incredible. Earthshaking. My whole body is vibrating and my center clenches around him. Despite my best attempts, a small whimper crawls out of my throat.

"Oh!" Axel gasps, his body seizing beneath me. His hands slide up my back, pulling down on my shoulders as if somehow, we could get any closer or he could get any deeper. He bursts inside me like his life depends on it.

Thank god I've got an IUD. Otherwise this would do the trick, no doubt.

I collapse over him, into his chest. All the anger dissipates for one moment and I accept his embrace. His closeness.

I missed this so much. His touch. His smell. Him.

Oh, Axel...

That's when the post-coital shame hits. Not just the general taboo feeling of sex that never seems to go away, but the fact that this should have never happened.

Though I'm wound in Axel's arms, I push myself off of him as if doing so isn't ripping me apart inside. As if my body hasn't taken me to seven years ago, to when my heart was beating to the sound of his. I can't do this. I've gone too soft. I must harden myself again.

"What are you doing?" he asks weakly.

I don't dare look at him. He probably looks so vulnerable laid out there in the chair. Softening, confused.

Needing me. Just as much as I need him.

No. He'd never need me or want me. Not now.

"That can't happen again," I say as I pull my pants back on. I run my hands through my hair, the waves feeling crazy and voluminous in my hands. I get the courage to turn back for him. He needs to hear this clearly. I'm not flinching away. "Not after what you did to me seven years ago."

Axel opens his mouth as if to respond and then shuts it.

"You should go. Now."

"Right. Uh." Axel hurriedly tucks himself away and gets up, smoothing out his suit jacket and pants errantly.

I feel him looking at me for something. But I have nothing else to say. Yes, that felt amazing. Which makes it even worse that it happened. How am I supposed to forget it when I know I must? For Lola's sake. For everyone's sake, really.

"Have a good night, Gillian."

I don't look up until I hear the door latch behind him. The room is empty. Just me and all the things that make up my life.

I'm filled with a sorrow I didn't expect. Because Axel had the chance to defend himself, to speak up for his actions from the past. And he didn't. If he had, maybe I would have finally told him the truth. A truth I have carried alone for the past seven years. A truth that may have the power to change everything.

I might have finally told him that the little girl sleeping in the other room isn't just mine.

She's his too.

Instead, he walked out of here just like he walks away from everything, proving every terrible thought I've had about him all this time.

Axel Hitchins is a coward and always will be.

6

———

AXEL

It's been a week. A whole goddamn week, and I can't get Gillian out of my head.

Obviously, this will not do. Not only is she the enemy to my whole livelihood, but she's my sister's best friend. It's always been an unspoken boundary. The death stares I got in our teen years when I told Gillian she looked nice were warning enough.

Although not enough to stay away completely.

It's time, though, to let the whole thing go. Sure, it was the best sex of my life, and *sure,* I wish we could do it again. And again. And again. But that's one hundred percent not going to happen, no way no how.

Right now, I'm on my way to meet Lola and Jeremiah. The three of us try to get lunch every few months and Jeremiah has just returned from Kenya. I'm sure he'll have lots of stories to tell us.

We meet at a trendy café on Sunset shrouded by monstera leaves and crowded with people wearing big sunglasses who would say they don't want to be recognized, yet definitely want to be recognized. As soon as I walk in, I spot Lola. I haven't seen her since before everything shook out with Gillian. Of course, when you tell yourself to not think about something, you're only going to be able to think about that. So, when I see my sister's face, my mind conjures Gillian's too.

Luckily, there's a distraction. Across from her, with his back to me, is my big brother, Jeremiah. Seeing him always makes me feel like a kid again. I wanted to be like him in every possible way. Now, we're adults and couldn't be more different.

Lola waves her hand, green eyes lighting up. "Ax! Over here!"

Jeremiah turns in his seat and smiles at me as I approach. His skin is tanner than it's ever been.

"I thought you'd be a walking sunburn!" I announce.

He stands and wraps his arms around me. I'm a tall guy and Jeremiah is even taller, gangly at six foot five. "There's the little guy!"

I laugh as he squeezes me. "Cut it out!"

Jeremiah releases me and then I go to Lola. "Hey, sis." I kiss the top of her head and try not to look at her too hard, or else my guilt might show on my face.

"Sit down, sit down. Jerry was just telling me about the time he had to stave off a lion with a torch." She's the only one of the family that can get away with calling Jeremiah by the nickname "Jerry". If I were to try, I'd be instigating a fight.

"Okay, that's putting it a little dramatically, don't you think?" Jeremiah chuckles.

"I'll be the judge of that," I say before motioning to the server approaching are table and mouthing, "Coffee."

Jeremiah regales us with a tale of being confronted with a lion in the middle of the night when he sleepily lost his way to the outhouse and nearly walked into a den. He has us in stitches, especially with the way he explains things, with wide eyes and crazy expressions. He's always such a goof. You'd think that job would fall on me as the younger brother, but he's always marched to the beat of his own drum.

"Okay, enough. I need to have my coffee. Jet lag. Tell me something," Jeremiah says, grabbing his iced latte and sipping. "How are things with you-know-who?"

I feel like I have a sword up to my throat. My mind immediately goes to Gillian.

"You mean *Dad?*" Lola says with a snort.

Thank god.

"Yeah, of course that's who I mean," Jeremiah says. The brightness of his smile fades.

"We don't have to talk about that if you don't want to," I say.

"No, I asked. I'd like to know since he, you know, doesn't talk to me anymore."

Lola and I exchange a look. Things with Jeremiah and Dad have been awful going on ten years. Started right when I graduated college and joined Jeremiah working under Dad at Hitchins. Jeremiah had already been there three years and, as the oldest son, was the assumed "heir" to the company. Dad had been showing him the ropes and he was hating every minute of it.

That's when all his do-gooder tendencies started. I guess he and Gillian have a lot in common that way. Started refusing to work on the bigger budget projects, especially in neighborhoods he perceived we were gentrifying. And then, came the big blow-up.

I remember standing outside of Dad's office door with Lola, listening to how they were going at each other. The gist was that Jeremiah wanted Hitchins to move away from luxury projects and into developments he saw as more impactful. Playgrounds, parks, "community spaces" (Man, he really is just like Gillian).

Dad didn't want anything to do with that and ousted him from the company. It was melodramatic. I think Dad did it to show Jeremiah just how willing he was to cut him off. If it had been me, I would have been immediately groveling at his feet.

But Jeremiah stuck to his guns. Left the company and took his own money to start funding projects in lesser developed nations. He was in Times' hundred most influential people just two years ago.

Dad and Jeremiah have never reconciled.

"Well, he's edgier than usual," Lola said with a look toward me. *You tell him.*

"The guy is seventy now, right? Makes sense he's starting to be a curmudgeon," Jeremiah said with a chuckle.

"It's worse than that," Lola continues. "Axel, tell him."

I frown incredulously. "Tell him what?!"

"You know, everything going on. With Gillian."

God, she doesn't even know what she's saying. "Everything going on with Gillian" includes a lot more than she could possibly begin to imagine. "Jeremiah doesn't want to hear about that," I say, clicking my tongue.

"Course I do. What's going on in the luxury property development game?" Jeremiah says with a cheeky waggle of his eyebrows. "You know, sometimes I miss it."

"Your nose just grew two feet."

Jeremiah grabs the end of his nose and laughs. "You're right. I'm lying. Now tell me, what's Gillian got to do with anything?"

I sigh heavily. *Lola...*the youngest. The most trouble.

God love her. "Well, the basic gist is we have some condos we're trying to build in Silver Lake."

"By the bakery," Lola says. "You need to stop by while you're in town, we've got a vegan éclair on the menu now that I want you to try."

"More importantly, it's by Gillian's daughter's school and it's apparently got all of this 'community heritage'. So, even though we own it–"

"She's protesting," Jeremiah finishes my sentence.

"Don't smile at that!"

His lips turn further up at the corners. "I'm not smiling!"

"Boys, please," Lola says in a calming tone. "Axel, keep going."

I close my eyes. I have explicitly told myself no more thoughts of Gillian, and yet, here I am, being forced to give a play by play of everything that's happened with her in the past two months. Well, almost everything. "She's not the only one protesting. She's got the whole neighborhood. People are down there nearly all hours of the day."

"Good for her."

"Whose side are you on?"

Jeremiah shrugs.

I grunt. He's such an ass when he wants to be. "We were supposed to break ground a month ago, and yet, here we are, stalled. Now the city council is all over it and–"

"Dad is up your ass to get it fixed."

"Stop doing that," I snap.

"What?!"

"Taking the words out of my mouth!"

"Guys!" Lola grabs each of us by the wrist this time. "Stop it!"

I glare at Jeremiah.

He holds up his hand in surrender. "I just know what that's like. Being the right-hand man. It might have only been a few years, but..."

I sigh. Maybe Dad's gone a bit easier on me than he did on Jeremiah. That says a lot considering Dad is a complete tyrant. But he's already lost one son to his temper. I know he misses Jeremiah, even if he doesn't say it. He'd have him back in his life in a heartbeat. Just...his pride is too powerful.

Guess I'm learning from the best.

"Anyway, you can only imagine how this is tearing *me* up," Lola pipes up, folding her arms over her chest.

"You and Gillian are good, though, right?" Jeremiah asks.

"As good as we can be when he's at her throat all the time."

I scoff. "She's at *mine* too."

"And when I'm with her, I let her know how much I don't like that! But right now I'm with you, so I'm going to give *you* shit for it."

Jeremiah looks across the restaurant, squinting his eyes, sun too bright. "What happened anyway? You guys used to be friends."

I open my mouth to reply, but Lola cuts me off. "We've been over this. They haven't gotten along for years."

"But why?"

Lola looks at me.

"Why are you looking at me?"

"Well, what'd you do?"

"Me? Nothing! We just–can't people not get along?!" I'm trying desperately to control the flush in my cheeks. I'm being cornered by the guilt, not just of betraying Lola last week, but seven years ago. That's when everything fell to shit between me and Gillian.

Lola looks to Jeremiah for sympathy. "It's been so hard on me, Jerry."

"I know, I can't even imagine," he replies. He puts a hand on her back and rubs it. Then, Jeremiah's eyes find mine. We all have the signature, matching green Hitchins eyes, just like Mom. "You know Axel's in a tough spot. This is the family's livelihood, Lola."

I smile at him gratefully.

"And Dad's not easy to please."

Lola huffs. "Tell me about it. He's starting to tell me my eggs are freezing up."

The three of us go quiet for a moment and look at each other with mournful eyes. Dad has never been easy to please, but things were better before Mom died. At least he smiled then.

"Lola, I'll handle it, okay?" I say encouragingly. "Whatever you can do to distract Gillian or get her to back off, great, but if not, I'm going to take care of it." Gillian's name nearly catches in my throat. My cover would be blown for sure if I started tripping over the consonants in her name. "And then we can all be done with this and go back to how things were."

Lola smiles at me. "You're the best, Axel."

My heart sinks into my stomach. I'm not the best. I'm the kind of guy who fucks his sister's best friend. And if she'd let me, I'd do it as often as I could, because I can't get enough of her, even all these years later, apparently, but that is my cross to bear.

For now, I'm done with the guilt trip over my job. Fuck it. I'm going to get this condo built once and for all. Be done with this feud. Be done with Gillian.

And though I know that's the right thing to do, the idea of being done with Gillian feels like a knife to my heart.

7

GILLIAN

"Just one more question, if you don't mind," the reporter asks, tucking a sprig of red hair into her messy bun.

"Perfect. Then I'll go take the brownies out of the oven," I say with a smile.

I'm being interviewed at the bakery by a local reporter trying to cover both sides of the issue over the Seton lot. She's trying to take a bipartisan approach and her questions have been tough but fair. I wasn't able to resist plying her with some free baked goods. A half-eaten vegan donut sits on a plate in front of her.

"Is your protesting making relations with your business partner, Lola Hitchins, difficult?"

I suck in my cheeks and glance at Lola who is working the counter, talking with a mother who is picking up a birthday cake.

"She is the younger sister of Axel Hitchins, who is helming this development, correct?"

At the sound of Axel's name, I snap my attention back to the reporter. "Yes. Yes, she is." I've got Axel on the brain morning, noon, and night. Nobody ever says the aftershocks of an orgasm can last days, but mine have lasted a whole week and change. I find myself daydreaming about him filling me, our lips fighting for dominance. On more than one occasion, Stella has had to snap me out of a trance. She's learned the best way to get my attention in times like those is to call me "Gillian" instead of "Mommy". Needless to say, I don't like how fast she's growing up.

I clear my throat. "It's funny to hear you call her a business partner. Lola and I were born a month a part. Our families were neighbors. Are still neighbors. We're best friends."

The reporter raises an eyebrow, holding her recorder up.

"Getting into business with your friends is hard. We've had knock down drag out fights over certain things. Even the style of chair you're sitting in right now." I clasp my hands. *Be careful...* "The protests over the Seton lot are my project and mine alone. I don't expect her to get involved. And, from my understanding, Axel's business..." *You didn't have to say his name, why did you fucking say his name,* "...is his business in the very same way. Just because they share the name doesn't mean she has to pick a side."

That's all I have to say on the subject. Sometimes, it drives me nuts that Lola won't just say, "Gillian, you're right." I know she believes in the things I believe. But she's under the thumb of her family. I can respect that.

My family would never make me choose, though.

"Thank you for your time, Ms. Solace."

"Of course, thank you for coming in. Now, let me get to those brownies."

LATER IN THE DAY, Lola and I are both behind the counter. It's slowing down, around four o'clock. Customers have learned our pastry case gets sad looking around this time.

We've got the radio playing, both doing our duties. Not really speaking except to work around each other.

I've been...quiet around her as of late. It's hard to look her in the eye when I've gone behind her back and done the one thing I'm not supposed to do.

Especially after I've already done it once before.

The song on the radio comes to an end and the host starts yammering. "Protests continue over the development of the Seton lot in Silver Lake."

Lola groans. "Not again."

I chuckle. "Sorry. You can turn it off if you want."

She glares at the radio and then shakes her head. "I can't help it, I'm curious."

"Axel Hitchins gave comment in interview with beat reporter, Brenda Collins," the host says.

"It's admirable," Axel's voice comes through the radio. I feel my body clam up. I haven't heard him speak since he was in my home, our bodies intertwined in forbidden lust. The sound makes me immediately wet. "But we know how this will end."

Even if I want to punch him in the face.

"Seton Elementary and the Silver Lake community do not have proprietary claim over the lot. The work-arounds that the protesters have found aren't substantial enough to make me worried."

"Do you have anything to say to Gillian Solace, leader of this movement?"

The blood leaves my face.

"Uh. No comment."

It was the best answer he could have given, and yet, it infuriates me beyond belief.

Suddenly, the radio turns off. I look back at Lola. "What'd you do that for?"

"Your knuckles are white," she says softly.

I look down at my hand clutching the wet rag I've been using to wipe up the counter. Sure enough, white as she said. I release the rag and unclench my hands. "Sorry."

"It's okay. I just don't want you getting worked up about it."

That's like telling water to stop being wet. Yet, she couldn't possibly know the depth of why I feel like this.

"You can talk about it, you know? I won't get upset," Lola says. She tries to remain as neutral as Switzerland on the issue, but she does lend an ear when she can.

But the things I need to say aloud...the things I've *never* said to anyone are things she can never know.

This has gone deeper than the protests at the Seton lot. This is now about me and Axel.

It was never supposed to happen, me and him. A mistake to the very core. Both of us going behind Lola's back while she was out of the country. We both swore up and down as soon as she returned that it would be over and done with and we wouldn't look back.

I never anticipated how badly he could hurt me. I've been holding onto that hurt for seven years now, waiting to be able to let it go.

How could I, though? He's going to be a part of my life until the day I die whether I like it or not.

Before we can talk about the protests, the door dings open and Stella leaps into the bakery. "Hello!"

"There she is! How was school?!" I come out from behind the counter and give her a great big hug.

"Good!"

Dana enters too, followed by Drew.

I look up at my older sister from my embrace with Stella. "Thanks for picking her up today."

"Any time. You know that," she smiles. "Hope you don't mind Drew tagged along. I promised him cookies."

Drew smiles sheepishly, scratching his brown beard. "I don't need cookies, Dana."

Of course he doesn't because it's a well-known fact that Drew has it bad for my sister. Okay, not a fact. No one has confirmed this. But there's definitely something going on there and I'm determined to get to the bottom of it.

"Well, you're in luck. We have some of those left. You want to take a look in the case?" Lola says, leaning onto the counter.

Drew heads over to take a look at what we have to offer.

"He's partial to oatmeal raisin which makes him a crazy person in my book," Dana says with a smile.

"Raisins? Yuck!" Stella remarks.

Drew shrugs. "More for me, then!"

I glance at Dana and see the smallest hint of a smile. If any of the Solace sisters deserve a man, it's her. She's been taking care of everyone for far too long. I know she loves doing it. She was basically our surrogate mother after Mom left. And she went into grief counseling as a career to take care of even *more* people. However, caretakers need to be taken care of too.

"Do you smell that?" Stella asks, sniffing wildly.

"Stella, don't blame other people if you tooted," I admonish.

"Not *that*! Gross!" she retorts. "It smells like—"

Dana's eyes widen. "Something is burning."

My heart drops into my stomach. "Oh no. the mixer."

I run into the kitchen and find the attachment on the industrial mixer whirring at top speed. Dough is flying across the room. Smoke is starting to form around the attachment. "Not again!" I cry out. I duck down trying to avoid the crossfire of dough and head straight toward the mixer. I know, basically a suicide mission.

I take hold of the power cord and pull on it with all my might until it comes out of the wall. The mixer makes a sound like a dying cat as it slows to a stop.

"You okay?" Lola calls out from the doorway.

I drop onto my bottom and sigh. "Fine. I think we might need to bite the bullet and get a new one of these."

"Sounds expensive," Dana remarks.

I turn around and find everyone piled into the doorway, including Stella. Though there is a feeling of dread in the room, she giggles. "Mommy, you've got dough in your hair."

I run my fingers through my loose blonde locks and find a splat of cinnamon dough. "Great, now I've gotta wash my hair."

"You mind if I take a look at it?" Drew pipes up from behind the girls.

We all look at him.

"Drew's an engineer, you know? He could help," Dana says encouragingly.

"Sure. She's all yours. Just be careful. Sometimes she sparks," I say, getting up to my feet and checking myself over for any more dough.

Drew laughs and crosses toward the mixer. "Don't worry, I've seen worse."

"There's no way we can afford a new one," Lola says with a sigh.

If only I hadn't started this drama with the Hitchins family, she might be able to ask her dad for a second loan.

We started the bakery five years ago, kickstarted by the Hitchins money. Stella was still under a year old, we were in our early twenties, trying to figure out how to make things work. And in comes Mr. Hitchins (I've never had the courage to call him by his first name, Paul).

Now, though, I'm sure he'd tell Lola to stick that question where the sun don't shine.

"Good thing is you won't need to!" Drew announces after not even a minute. "It's just some faulty wiring. I can fix it no problem."

"Seriously?" I ask.

Drew nods. "You bet."

"What's your rate?" I ask.

He frowns. "Uh, free."

"No way," Lola says. "No way, there's no way."

"Okay, you know what, fine," Drew says. "A dozen oatmeal raisin. I won't go lower."

I shake my head, about to rebut, but Dana intercedes. "He's doing it for free, Gillian."

"No, he's doing it for a dozen oatmeal raisin! If you can start tomorrow, I'll double it!" Lola says with a grin, bouncing over to Drew and throwing her arms around him with gratitude.

I look at Dana with relief. She smiles, holding her hands up. I'm going to have to have a talk with her. She's got to nail down this man as soon as possible. He's too good to lose.

Another sister to be jealous of...

"Mommy..." Stella comes up beside me and grabs my hand. "Can we go home now? I'm tired."

I smile down at her, though my heart lurches when our eyes meet.

I'm never going to be able to forget him, am I?

"Of course. Let me just get cleaned up. And then we'll

go home." It might be nice to have a man to go home to. Someone to help with the bills and school pickups. However, if the family I have the rest of my life is just Stella and me, I know that's a life well-lived.

She's my whole heart. No one else.

8

———

AXEL

I hate galas. Or to be more specific, I hate schmoozing. Because that's all it is. A bunch of rich people in some hotel ballroom somewhere all rubbing elbows and laughing with each other, even though we all hate each other's guts.

I've been forced into this by my dad. I have five events like this over the next month I'm attending in his stead in order to smooth things out regarding the Seton lot issue.

The funny thing about these people is that they're the ones who are going to buy these condos. But they can't stand the idea of being looked at as unkind or unpitying. They want to have their condo and also look like they care about the community. So that means, Hitchins has to pay by showing up and explaining to everyone how our luxury condominiums are going to improve the neighborhood.

Spoiler alert, it's not.

Silver Lake is already one of the most expensive areas in LA. Another luxury apartment complex is just a blip on the landscape.

Yet, here we are.

I'm on my third whisky of the night. The programming for the night included a dinner and some sort of ceremony honoring top donors to a music program for underprivileged kids. I nearly vomited hearing people crying while a boy from Compton went to town on a Chopin number. He was great. The virtue signaling, not so much.

Although part of the reason I'm here is to be honored for a humongous donation Hitchins has just made toward the program. Talk about virtue signaling.

Now, I'm just biding my time, waiting it out. Dad said I had to stay until eleven and it's currently a quarter to. I can make it. I can definitely make it if I just don't make eye contact.

I feel a tap on my arm. "Mr. Hitchins!"

I turn around and find a woman who must be at least fifteen years older than me, draped in velvet and skin pulled so tight I wonder how much of her face is original.

She pats my cheek. "Have you gotten some work done, Paul?" she asks, clearly making a joke.

"Oh, I'm afraid you've got the wrong Hitchins," I say, forcing a smile. "I'm Axel, his son."

She gasps playfully. "Axel Hitchins? So grown up already! It's not possible."

I must have met this woman before.

"I bet you don't even remember me."

"Of course I do."

She shakes her head and holds out her hand for me to take. "Linda Drosney."

Of the Drosney fortune...of course. I take her hand and begin to shake it, but she has other ideas. She engulfs my hand in both of hers and pulls herself closer. "I met you and your father at the Philharmonic several years ago. Does that ring a bell?"

Oh god, I don't like this. "Yes, it does."

"Good. Good." She leans in even closer. This is fight for fuck territory. I'm certainly not going to punch this woman for standing too close, but I'll be damned if she thinks I'm going to kiss her either. "I've been watching you standing here alone, waiting for your wife to come join you."

"Oh," I say, flustered. "No wife. Just me."

Linda rubs my hand. "Yes, I can feel that now."

She must mean my ring finger, but the way she says it makes me feel sick to my stomach.

"I'm recently divorced."

"I'm sorry to hear that."

She guffaws. "Don't be! You should be saying congratulations. Because that's what it is! A congratulations."

I chuckle lightly. "Well, then congratulations."

Linda beams. "Thank you, Axel. That means a lot coming from you."

I'm not sure why, unless that's her lame attempt at a flirtation. "Any time," I reply with a curt nod, then take a sip of my whisky to put a pin at the end of this conversation.

However, that's not an overt enough signal to Linda Drosney. She tilts her head to the side, glancing over her shoulder, before fixing her eyes on me again. Like a cat, her pupils widening as if fixated on her prey. "You're too handsome to be at something like this alone."

I force a smile. "Oh, well, thank you."

"You're welcome."

"So, no wife. No girlfriend?"

"Would that matter?" I grumble under my breath. The term "girlfriend" or "boyfriend" in Southern California is as meaningless as calling someone a buddy or pal. To some people, it means *absolutely nothing* if it stands in the way of what they want. The only reason Linda Drosney would care is in the case we might be interrupted, and she'd have to walk away with egg on her face.

She raises an eyebrow or tries to. The Botox makes it nearly impossible for her to move her forehead. "Beg your pardon?"

"Nothing, sorry, frog in my throat." I clear my throat and then smile.

Linda smiles back, none the wiser to my comment. "What are you doing after this?"

My heart sinks into my stomach. I glance down subtly at my watch. Six minutes. Literally six minutes until I can leave this godforsaken event and I'm being hounded by an aging heiress looking for a date. "Um, well, it's a Thursday—"

"I can't imagine days of the week really matter to someone like you. You take after your father, don't you?"

I grimace. In his heyday, Dad certainly was a bit of a party animal. After Mom passed away and before he got his hip replaced. "You know, in a lot of ways, I do," I say, a queasy feeling coming over me. Turning into my father one day at a time. Someone stop me, please. "But unlike him, I really do like my beauty sleep."

Linda takes a sip of her martini and then smiles, lips glistening with vodka. "Mm, I can tell."

I swallow and look around. The event has started to thin out just a bit. I'd like to be a part of that mass exodus primly at eleven o'clock.

"You're young, I think you can afford to live a little. That's what my kids tell me."

Jesus Christ. This woman is talking to me about her kids. Kids old enough and sentient enough to give her quips and witticisms. Textbook definition of a cougar. Listen, I don't knock it for some people. But older women, at least *substantially* older women, have never been my cup of tea. "How old are your kids?" I ask, unable to contain my curiosity.

"Well, Brandon's twenty-four–"

I nearly spit out my drink.

"And Keely is twenty-two–"

I'm starting to feel faint.

"And Frankie just turned eighteen! He's the only one still at home with me, but he's off to college in September."

This woman might just be looking for a fling, but if she wants more than that, she sees me as a prospective stepfather to three *grown adults*. "How old do you think I am, Ms. Drosney?"

Her eyes bug out. "Please! Linda. Call me Linda."

I take a deep breath. "Linda."

"Better." She grabs my arm and then leans away from me, taking in my stature and appearance with a critical eye that would be better used for identifying constellations or translating lost languages. Then, she leans toward me, closer than she should. I try to be polite and not duck away from her like she's diseased, but her breath is soiled with alcohol and is making my insides curdle. "*Young.*"

Well, that couldn't have been a creepier answer.

"How old do you think *I* am?"

I laugh. "I know better than that."

She shakes her head and pulls herself into me, our hips nearly touching. "I'm asking, though. There's a difference."

I look into her yellow-brown eyes, examine her skin pulled taught like a drum, her duckish lips, and her auburn hair, clearly dyed and highlighted to hide any trace of gray. "Young."

Linda's eyes widen; she throws her head back with laughter, leaning into me. I laugh too, awkwardly, looking around to see if anyone is looking at us thinking what a strange pair we must be. Although, I guess that's a fallacy in my head. In LA, there's no such thing as a strange pair. Especially not when it comes to age.

"Axel Hitchins, you are..." Her hands slide up my arms to my shoulders. "Absolutely charming."

I chew on my lower lip nervously.

"Let's get out of here."

"I can't tonight."

"I'll give you my number. We can arrange something this weekend. So I can have you all night."

I try not to let the terror read on my face, but no way no how am I allowing Linda Drosney to *have me all night.* That sounds like a recipe for disaster. "Look, Ms. Drosney–"

"Linda."

"*Linda*, I really appreciate your offer. I'm very flattered, but–"

"Don't think I don't know when I'm being rejected, Axel. I've been around the block before," she says, but she makes no effort to draw away. "The thing is, I can be very convincing."

I glance down at my watch again. Fuck it's a minute past eleven. And I'm still stuck here. "The things is..."

"What's 'the thing', Axel?" she asks, baby-talking me, pressing her front onto mine.

My body swells with alarm bells. I need to get out of this, I need to do it quick. "I have feelings for someone else," I blurt.

Though it comes out without any thought, an image attaches to it right away. A person that I'm not sure where I stand with nor how I really feel. But she's there in my brain all the same.

Gillian.

Linda guffaws. "Feelings? This doesn't have to be anything about feelings, Axel."

"Well, I don't think I would be respecting myself or–or this person if I were to–"

"You're so adorable when you're nervous."

I try to spew out some more words to defend myself, but Linda has made up her mind and she's too quick for me to dodge. She throws herself at me, lips colliding with mine messily. It's the clumsiest kiss I've ever had the displeasure of being a part of. I push her away by the shoulders and wipe my mouth off with the back of my hand. "Linda, really, I–"

"Oh, don't be shy, Axel!"

She goes in for another kiss and I duck away again, this time leaping several feet away from her. "No! Thank you, but I–I–" I glance around to see if anyone is watching. No one seems plussed by it. But there is a photographer just nearby looking down at his camera screen, clicking through photos. God, did he... I can't think about that right now. "I have to go."

Linda calls out after me, but I can't hear the words she says. My blood is boiling and the only thing keeping back the torrent of my ire is that I *have* to be a good boy in public, so my fucking *dad* doesn't get a phone call about me. I'm thirty-two years old and I still have to act correctly lest I embarrass my father and the Hitchins name.

Luckily for me, my driver is waiting right out front. I asked him to meet me at eleven and hate to have kept him waiting. I leap in, slam the door after me, and let out a heavy sigh.

"Everything alright, Mr. Hitchins?"

I glance up at the driver and shake my head. "Just take me home."

The driver doesn't say another word, just puts the car into gear and starts to drive. I immediately feel relief wash over my body as we leave Linda Drosney in the rearview mirror.

However, the whole ride home, I'm plagued with what I said. "I have feelings for someone else." And the image I conjured of Gillian in my mind.

That can't be true. I just have her on the brain nonstop since we slept together. That doesn't mean I have *feelings* for her. Besides, the only communication we've had over the past seven years has been nothing but forced politeness and consternation. There's no reason for me to feel anything for her at all.

But if I don't have feelings, more than intense loathing that leads to passion, why is it so damn hard not to think about her?

9

GILLIAN

"Three éclairs, coming up!" I say to my latest customer. I got to bag up her order, but nearly drop one éclair on the ground when I hear a loud clatter from the kitchen.

I glance at my customer. Her eyes are wide with fright. "Sorry about that. We're having some work done on our mixer and–"

Another crash.

I force a smile and hurriedly hand her the bag of éclairs. "Next time you come in, I promise it won't be–"

One more impossibly tremendous bang. Just for good measure.

"— a problem," I finish sheepishly.

The customer thanks me and scurries out of the bakery faster than I can say "goodbye."

I sigh. The noise has been pretty constant all day since Drew arrived to fix the mixer. Bless his heart, I know we're getting the repairs for free, but the man is noisy. We usually get some customers who like to hang around and linger, but as I look around, all the café tables are empty. And I'm starting to get a migraine.

Deep breath, Gillian. Don't bite the hand that feeds you.

I go to the front door and flip the sign from open to closed. I need a little bit of a break.

I grab a couple cans of sparkling water and an oatmeal raisin cookie and bring it all into the back. Drew is bent over in the corner, his entire back drenched in sweat.

"Hey," I say.

Drew jumps, knocking his head against the back of the mixer. "Ow! Fuck!"

"Sorry! I didn't mean to scare you."

Drew grits his teeth but doesn't curse me out even though I'd deserve it. "It's okay, I should have been more careful," he says, rubbing the back of his head.

I hold up the sparkling water and cookie. "Thought you might need a break."

He glances at the mixer and then sighs. "I'm nearly done, but yeah. Yeah, that'd be nice."

With many thanks, he takes the sparkling water, but his sights are set on the cookie. He devours it in less than a minute.

"You want another?"

"No, no, I shouldn't," he says sheepishly and then cracks the can open. "Mm. Thank you. Needed this."

I perch on the edge of one of the metal tables. "Thanks for doing this, Drew."

He hums. "That's about the fourteenth time you've said that."

"Well, it bears repeating."

Drew leans against the mixer and heaves a sigh. "I'm happy to do it, Gillian. Believe me."

I can't help the corner of my mouth turning upward in a mischievous smile. "You're a really nice guy."

He shrugs. "I'm not all that."

"Stop, don't be so modest. I know we're all grateful Dana has you."

Drew's eyes alight slightly. *Shit.*

"You know, you two are such good friends."

He looks away. "Yeah. I'm lucky to have her too. Not often your grief counselor turns into your best bud."

The way he says bud is definitely stilted. I've never been truly alone with Drew. I don't think any of us have been. Other than Dana of course. This could be my chance to get to know him a bit better. Maybe get a read on if he has any feelings for my sister. "Have you ever thought about...I don't know..."

Drew smirks. "Gillian, you're not slick, okay?"

My eyes widen. "What do you mean?"

"I'm not an idiot. Well. Not all the time." He takes a long sip of his seltzer and then exhales. "I see how you and your sisters are always glancing at each other when you're around Dana and me. And I hate to break it to you, but nothing is happening between us."

Oh, I know that. Dana wouldn't keep it a secret. At least I don't think she would. Even if she didn't give us all the details, I'd hope she'd let us know that something was finally (finally!) happening between the two of them. "Does that mean you don't *wish* there was something happening?"

Drew's eyes connect with mine; there's the smallest tic in his cheek as if he's trying to decide whether he's going to tell the truth or bend it just a little. "Gillian–"

"If you don't answer, Drew, that's as good as an answer. You know what I mean?"

He rests his forearms on his knees and sighs. "You promise not to say anything?"

Jackpot. "Promise." Too bad he doesn't know my fingers are crossed behind my back. No way I'm not telling at least *one* of my sisters.

"I can see your fingers crossed behind your back, Gillian."

Dammit.

Drew laughs. "Remember. Not slick."

I drop my hand and sigh. "Okay. Fine. I won't tell anyone. Promise. Capital 'p'."

He frowns.

"It's something Stella and I do. If it's a promise with a capital 'p', it's a big one."

"You two are so cute together. A dynamic duo."

I smile, though my heart sinks. Yes, we're a dynamic duo. But shouldn't we be a terrific trio? Mom, baby, *and* dad? I shake it off. "Anyway..."

"Okay, well ,as long as you're not telling..." Drew trails off. "I'm interested in Dana."

I clap my hands together and squeal.

"But! You know, it's never going to happen."

I gape at him. "How can you say that like it's a fact?"

"Because she's got her shit and I've got mine and–"

"That's the whole point of being in a relationship with other people. Dealing with each other's shit."

Drew laughs and nods. "Maybe, but...we're too good of friends. I don't want to spoil that."

My heart sinks. I remember when I was too good of friends with someone, and I didn't want to spoil what we had between us. Axel and me. And yet, one drink too many, one shy kiss, and bam. Seven years of disdain. Friendship ruined by horny brain cells. It's not worth it in the end. "I get it. It can ruin everything."

"Right? Exactly. You get it."

Do I ever.

"I can't lose her because I wanted to risk making our relationship anything more than it already is. You know?"

It breaks my heart because I totally understand where he's coming from. And I also know just how perfect they'd be together. But being inside something like that is terrifying. You can never believe a person on the outside saying that everything logistically adds up and that you'd be a perfect pair. You have to feel it.

"Plus, I don't think she even notices me."

"What?! That's crazy."

"I mean, she doesn't really notice when I flirt or–"

I scoff. "That's just Dana. She's always in her own head."

"I wouldn't say that. She's just focused on the things that matter most to her. Her family, her job."

I smile at him. "Her friends."

Drew laughs lightly. "Her friends. Sure."

We are both quiet for a long moment. I don't really know what to say. Without knowing how Dana feels, I can't really push him to make a move. And also, having been on the other side of ruining a friendship, I sympathize with his plight.

"Things are just fine the way they are right now," Drew says firmly. "I'd rather have Dana in my life like this than not at all."

Damn, this man is so romantic. It makes me want to scream. When is it my turn?

"You're a good egg, Drew," I say.

He scratches his hand through the scruff on his cheek.

"I'm alright. Okay. I should get back to work and then get out of your hair."

"You're the best," I say with a smile.

"I'm not–"

"Take the damn compliment!"

He laughs. "Aright, alright."

I start to leave the kitchen but stop when my phone buzzes in my pocket. Text from Fran. Jesus...I don't know if I can take this right now. Any talk of the Seton lot right now sends my thoughts right toward Axel and where there are thoughts of Axel there are thoughts of our bodies entangled in my living room and where there are thoughts of –

My brain goes blank when I open her text.

It's a picture. Of Axel Hitchins. Wearing a perfectly tailored suit and looking finer than I'd like to admit.

Around his neck hangs an auburn-haired beauty.

And...they're kissing.

A text appears under the picture.

> Competition trying to repair their image by literally sucking up.

Followed by a series of eye roll and expletive faced emojis.

Another text.

> Pathetic.

I don't have words. And I know better than to scroll back up and look at the picture. But curiosity is getting the best of me.

I look at the picture until I'm frowning so hard my forehead might stay like that.

So, not only is he going to try and thwart me at every

turn but he's going to suck face with a glamorous heiress or businesswoman or whoever the fuck? Right after we—not that it meant anything, but –

Why is my heart breaking? Why am I feeling like this? I hate him, don't I?

I clench my phone in my hand and feel my hands start to shake. "God fucking *dammit*."

"What's wrong? You okay?"

I turn around, remembering Drew is still in the room with me. I try to smile. "Oh, you know. Just have to curse every now and then to get that negative energy out. Namaste, etc."

Drew frowns, but nods. "Makes sense."

"Sorry," I mutter and then go back to the front of the bakery. Always easy to pass off my weird quirks as hippy dippy behavior. Gotta take the wins when I can.

I bury my phone away in the bottom of the register. If it's out of sight, maybe it can be out of mind.

But no matter how hard I try not to think about it, I keep getting that image of Axel's lips entangled with someone else's. Someone more beautiful, more worldly, more suited for him.

By the end of the day, I feel sick to my fucking stomach.

10

————

AXEL

"This...this is good work, son."

I stare at the computer screen. My dad is pointing to an article written by the LA Times. A nothing, puff piece talking about the gala I was at just two days ago.

They just happened to have used a photo of me and Linda Fucking Drosney in a collage for the article. And yes, our lips are literally locked. It's giving me war flashbacks just looking at it.

"Didn't know you had a penchant for older women."

I glare at my father. He has a shit-eating grin on his face. "I don't." I collapse back into my seat across from him at his desk. It's a beautiful Saturday. Gorgeous. Perfect weather for surfing or sailing. Instead, I'm locked in yet another conversation with my father about what the hell we are going to do about managing media around the Seton lot.

Apparently, me getting cornered by an older woman is "good work".

"And a Drosney at that..." he continues cheekily.

"Look, Dad, it was...she was drunk. I was just trying to go. She was lonely, wanted some attention, I–"

"You sound embarrassed. Don't be embarrassed! Now everyone is going to be going around town talking about you and Linda Drosney. That's going to take all the heat off the Seton lot. They're going to be asking questions like 'isn't she so much older than him' and 'didn't she just get divorced', all the while the city council quietly comes to a decision and then we are in the clear."

I frown. "In the clear?"

Dad smiles even more. "Drosney's father is a city councilman."

"Jesus, how old is he?"

Dad furrows his brow. "Old men can still get the job done."

"What I mean is—I just thought she—"

"Please, she's not much older than you."

I give him an incredulous look. "She has two kids in their twenties."

Dad grumbles, "I said not *much* older than you."

I shake my head. "Well, I'm so happy that my trauma has taken the heat off of you, Father."

"Trauma?! You're being dramatic."

I lean back in my chair and glance out the window. Yes. Beautiful spring day. I sit up a little straighter when I hear the voice of one of the Solace girls outside. Harley, I think, by the brash laughter that follows.

"Now, listen, I'm proud of you. You're getting out there, you're doing damage control. That's exactly what we need to be doing right now. So here."

I glance at my father. He's holding out a business card. I frown, taking it from him. "What's this?"

He doesn't say anything.

I scan the card, immediately my face drops. Linda Drosney. It's her fucking card. "How'd you get this?"

"She sent it over. By courier. Taken a shine to you."

I blink at him.

"I want you to call her."

I can't hold back my laughter. "Call her?"

Dad crosses his arms over his chest and gruffly grunts. "What's wrong with that?"

"I can't–I –" I stand up and start to pace. "I can't *call* her, Dad. Then she'll think I'm interested in her."

"Yes! That would be the point, wouldn't it?"

I stop short and stare at him.

"Her *father* is a city *councilmember*. I know math has never been your strong suit, Axel, but–"

"You want me to pretend to date her, so the city council *maybe* grants us the permission to continue the build?"

"Precisely."

I feel like I've been plunged underwater, the world around me going mute and slow motion. I need a moment. To think.

This is...low. Even for my dad.

I stare down at the card and then look up through the window once more. Now, I can get a good look at the back-yard. All the Solace sisters are congregating together. Saturday brunch. How cute.

I can't help but look for Gillian. Kent at the head of the table, flanked by Harley holding her new baby and Dana, then Kira and Amy, but no–"

"We're here!" I hear Stella squeal so loud she might as well be in the room with me, not outside. She bounds into view, greeting all her aunts and grandfather with gusto.

I smile to myself.

And where Stella goes, Gillian isn't far behind. She strolls in toting a bohemian satchel (no doubt vegan leather). Her long dirty blonde tresses look perfectly tousled by the wind, and though she moves slowly with the exhaustion of a single mother, it's so elegant and poised.

Why does she have to be so beautiful? Why can't she be a hideous monster instead of an absolute goddess that I can't help but –

"Axel!" my father grouses, interrupting my daydream.

I turn back to my father, leaving the window and all daydreaming of Gillian Solace behind me. "Sorry?"

"You'll do it, won't you?"

I know I should just do it. Suck it up. How long could I have to keep up the charade. A couple months at most? The decision will come soon enough. All I have to do is pretend like it wasn't for the sole purpose of getting our building permits and then I'll be able to move on from Linda Drosney, just like I've moved on from every other woman in my life.

She may have crossed the line with me, but even she doesn't deserve that kind of disrespect.

"Don't you think that's going too far, Dad?"

He chuckles. "We have to get this built, son."

"Sure, but...that's...I'm not willing to go that far."

The light doesn't change in the room, but a shadow passes over my dad's face. He just has this uncanny ability to create darkness out of nowhere. It's terrifying. I used to admire it. Now, though, on the other side of it, I just want to run away. "What do you mean you're not willing to go that far?"

"I just mean–"

"Axel, this is our empire. Our legacy."

Oh god, he's launching into a movie villain monologue.

"You really are just going let it fall to pieces because you're not willing to do what needs to be done?"

I open my mouth to reply.

"Maybe I was wrong about you."

A stinging sensation hits my chest. "What?"

"That you were more capable of following in my footsteps than your brother." My dad turns his attention to his computer monitor and errantly clicks around as if he doesn't have the time of day for me. "What a disappointment."

"I *am* capable, Dad."

He is silent. Ignoring me.

I might be thirty-two years old, but he has a way of making me feel like a mere child. Ignoring me, making it clear I have expectations to live up to, giving me a disappointed look when I haven't fulfilled my obligation to him as my father.

Why have children if you're expecting them to be anything but your own person?

"I don't feel comfortable. That's all. I'll keep going to events, I'll schedule some dinners, I'll even –"

"That's not good enough!" he barks.

I wince, words cutting me deep. Mom just wanted us to be good people. Jeremiah would make her proud. Lola too. Now here I am, being berated by our father who wants me to fake date someone just to get a condo built.

What have I become?

Dad takes a deep breath and rubs his eyes. "I don't want it to go this way, Axel."

"Which way?"

He raises his gray eyes to mine. They are cold and distant. Is that what people see in me? I remember when his eyes were tinged always with a smile. Now, this man isn't my dad. He's my boss. "I'm good at giving an ultimatum, Axel. You know I follow through on my word."

My insides tremble. He's seriously suggesting cutting me out. Just like he did Jeremiah. That would just leave

Lola. And who is to say he wouldn't eventually cut her out too. This man doesn't know what it means to care. What it means to love.

At least not anymore.

"Hm? What do you have to say, Axel?"

I purse my lips.

What the hell is my life even? What does it mean?

"I need a moment," I say softly.

Dad's face twists with disgust. Though he doesn't say it aloud, I can hear what he's thinking. *Soft. You're so fucking soft.*

I leave without another word, quietly walking the halls of my childhood home. A place that used to be my haven. Now it feels wretched.

My head swirls with thoughts as I get out to the car. I've given everything to my family. I have worked my ass off for years, avoiding any distractions. I've convinced myself I haven't wanted relationships or a family of my own because that is what pleased my father.

And yet, one wrong move and he wants to cut me out.

At least I'd have Jeremiah.

I settle in behind the wheel of my beamer and lean back. I need to go for a drive. A long one.

I've got to clear my head.

11

———————

GILLIAN

"I forgot the donuts, give me one second!" I shout over my shoulder as I head back to the driveway to my car. Always a little bit scatter-brained. I'd say that's motherhood for you, but I've always been a little bit like this. Before I get to my car, I see Axel's car pulling out of their driveway. It squeals onto the pavement. Then, he floors it, burning rubber down the residential street.

I ought to call the cops on him. Who does he think he is driving around here like that? Children play on these streets. They could get hurt.

Who am I kidding, though? Axel hasn't ever given a shit about anyone but Axel in a long time.

"Can I help?"

My gaze shoots to Harley who is standing at the gate waiting for me.

"You're not supposed to be helping anyone. You're supposed to *rest*," I chide, reaching into my car and grabbing the plastic container of French-toast-inspired donuts.

Harley leans up against the gate and smiles. "It's nice to get a moment away now and again."

I sigh. "I remember that feeling."

"Am I bugging you? I know I've been leaning on you a lot lately."

My mouth falls ajar. "Are you kidding?" I go up to my younger sister and wrap my arm around her. "You're never bugging me."

"You didn't use to say that," she grins.

I roll my eyes. "Yeah, well, that's before you grew up."

"Hey!" She elbows me in the side.

I jerk away and laugh. I deserved that one.

"Why do you always have to bring baked goods? It's already been hard enough to lose the weight."

I roll my eyes. "You're one month postpartum."

"Yeah, but–"

"You're young. It'll come off. Promise." We stop walking at the end of the path that leads to the backyard, allowing us to have a few more seconds of privacy. "You still have a baby to feed, Harley. And you're recovering."

She smiles and looks down at her shoes. "I know, it's just...harder than I want it to be."

Harley and I talk a lot. Like nearly on the daily. She always has questions about what's normal and when she needs to be worried. "Her feet are purple! What's going on?" or "I just put her down and she's hungry again! I feel like a cow!" or "Will I ever want to have sex again?"

I remember asking all those questions. Except I had to pop them into google. Found a lot of good mom friends on forums and eventually at daycare. I'm always happy to lend an ear, even if I'm smiling to myself, just trying to convince Harley that most of the weirdness is as to be expected when it comes to being postpartum and taking care of a newborn.

"Remember, Tana's happy when you're happy. She can

sense it. Doesn't mean you have to keep it up all the time, but you feed each other's energies," I explain.

Harley groans. "It's like I made her or something."

I laugh. "Exactly."

"Thank you. For making me feel normal."

I touch my sister on the cheek. "Always."

We both take a deep breath and round the corner to the backyard where the rest of the family is waiting: our sisters, Dad holding baby Tana, and, of course, Stella. "Okay, as promised –"

"Ooh! These look amazing, Gilly!" Dana announces, taking the case from me and setting it down on the table amongst many other delectable dishes. A platter of bacon, beautiful ripe berries, cinnamon buns. This is a food coma waiting to happen.

I see Stella already has a whole cinnamon roll in her hand. "Who told you that you could start?"

"Aunt Kira," Stella says with a mouthful of dough, eyeing Kira nervously.

Kira's eyes dart to the side behind her glasses. She shrugs.

"It's always the quiet ones," Dad says. Tana then squalls in response and Dad smiles. "And you're definitely not one of the quiet ones."

I see Harley's face drop out of the corner of my eyes. She was just able to pawn the baby off on Dad and she's already in need of some coddling. As good as Dad is at soothing babies, Tana is definitely a mommy's girl. "Let me have her," I say and go to my dad. "I want a try."

"Really, Gillian, just let me–" Harley starts to protest but I wave her off.

"I want to try. I have done this before, you know?" I take little Tana up in my arms. Still so soft and tiny, face still just slightly scrunched. And with just a few little bounces, she quiets down, settling onto my shoulder. "There you go."

"I think she just hates men," Amy says.

"That's not true!" Dad replies defensively while the rest of us giggle.

"You guys start. I'm just going to make sure she settles down," I say softly, rubbing Tana's back.

No one objects; they all begin loading their plates. Harley settles back into her seat and mouths a thank you to me while I walk back and forth, bouncing Tana in my arms. She smells...so good. Brings me right back to the early days of Stella. We were still strangers and we were both so confused, but we had each other.

We will always have each other.

"So, I know you've been busy, Harley, but have you given any more thought to the wedding?" Dana asks.

Harley laughs tiredly and nods. "Yes. Courthouse. End of next month. *Simple.*"

"Do you hear that? The lady wants *simple*," Kira says, glaring at Amy.

"Yeah, simple!" Stella adds.

I laugh, continuing to pace. "Did Amy have a few too many grandiose ideas?"

"It'd be criminal for them not to have a real wedding!" then looking at Grant, she adds, "You two are so beautiful together. And you're rich, so–" Amy explains.

Harley hums knowingly. "Even money can't convince me to have a big, pain in the ass kind of wedding."

"I have no objections to that," Dad murmurs. Dana pokes him on the arm and gives him a look. The two of them have their own language, since she stepped into Mom's place. That look said, "Don't be a cynic."

"More importantly," Harley goes on. "We don't want to

wait. We want to be married as soon as possible and focus entirely on Tana." She looks at me with suddenly desperate eyes. I know that look well. When you're a mother to a newborn, all you want is a second to yourself. But the moment you have it, you need to get your hands on your baby again.

I giggle and hand Tana back to Harley. My sister gapes at me. "She's out cold! How did you do that?"

"She's had practice!" Stella echoes from earlier.

"I'm sorry, is there a parrot in here?" Dad asks playfully.

"Caw-caw!" my daughter responds.

I laugh and settle in beside her, wrapping her into a hug. My little baby. Not so much a baby anymore. Where is the time going?

"But I wouldn't say no to big party," Harley says devilishly.

"*That* we can definitely manage," Amy grins.

We start talking about the details of Harley and Grant's reception, a big party to be held on one of the Infinium lots. We discuss themes (settling on carnival mostly because that's what Stella was most excited about) and food ("Corn-dogs, obviously," is Harley's answer). It's definitely going to be...unique, I'll say that. In tune with the theme, I start dreaming up different sweet treats I could make. Funnel cakes, elephant ears, deep fried Oreos. This is going to be fun.

Toward the end of our brunch, we hear someone call out from the gate, "Are we interrupting?"

Amy's eyes immediately shoot toward the source of the voice which then leads me to recognize it too. Hunter Ricks, the new neighbor.

"Not at all! Come on back, Hunter!"

"*Dad!*" Amy hisses.

Dad holds his hands up innocently.

Hunter is Amy's nemesis, but I'm not sure she's his. Ever since he moved in, his schedule and habits seem to get in the way of her creative process. His only saving grace in her eyes is–

"Jessica!" Amy yelps at the sight of Hunter leading his little girl into the yard by the hand.

Jessica is three years old, desperately shy, cute as a button with long dark hair just like her dad, fringed at the forehead, and dimples when she smiles. Somehow, Amy makes her come out of her shell.

That doesn't surprise me, though. Amy has always been good with children.

"I, uh, have a gift for Harley and..."

"Tana!" Jessica squeaks to her father.

"Tana, right. Sorry," Hunter says with an awkward smile. It's almost comical when he's unsure of what to say. The man is tall, dark, and handsome, almost like Jason Momoa but even better somehow. If he were my type, I would have snatched him up ages ago, but alas. I go for the more anemic doltish types ala Axel Hitchins, *apparently*.

Harley smiles. "Oh, Hunter, you didn't have to do that."

"It's nothing much," he says humbly and then crouches down to Jessica's height. "Here, you want to give it to her?"

Jessica nods and takes the long box from her father. She toddles over toward Harley and holds it up over her head.

"Wow, thank you for carrying it all the way over here," Harley says. "I can tell Tana already loves it."

Dad takes the box and puts it on the table for Harley to open.

"Uh, Amy, could I speak with you for just a moment?" Hunter asks casually, nodding his head away from the table.

We all look at Amy. *Oooh...you're in trouble.*

She nervously looks around at us, brushing her long brown curls off of her face. "Um. Yeah. Sure."

She leaps out of her chair and joins him over by the pool. I can tell she's nervous because she's clasping and unclasping her hands repeatedly.

"What's that about?" I ask.

Dana shrugs and shakes her head.

"He's been finding reasons to talk to her more often lately," Kira says matter-of-factly.

"Oh, would you look at this!" Harley exclaims. "Matching pajamas! For me and for Tana?"

Jessica nods heavily, looking at her dad and Amy over her shoulder.

"Thank you so much," Harley smiles.

Jessica looks down at her feet, swaying her body left and right, blushing heavily.

I lean over and whisper in Stella's ear. "Hey, could you–"

"Jessica, do you want to play on the teeter totter?" Stella cries out, leaping out of her seat. That kid. Too smart for her own good sometimes. She knew what I was going to say before I even said it.

Stella grabs Jessica's hand and the two little ones race over to the teeter totter.

"Thank god, I thought I was going to make her burst into tears," Harley says with a sigh of relief.

Everyone starts chatting while I watch Hunter and Amy by the pool. The conversation looks somewhat intense, but maybe that's just Hunter's permanently furrowed brow. Amy's lips curl to the side. Thinking. Then she nods and says something. Hunter's frown breaks for a moment and he smiles. A grin, actually. He leans in. Is he about to hug her?

But then he stops short and holds out his hand for her to shake.

When they return, Hunter gives us all an awkward nod. "Anyway, sorry to interrupt. Congratulations again, Harley. Unless I didn't say it before, but–"

"Thank you. I love the pajamas."

"I know they're big. But it'll be something she can grow into. Time flies when they're so small." He glances over at Jessica and Stella.

"You sound just like Gillian!" Harley exclaims.

I shrug. "It's the truth."

"Yes, well, anyway. We'll get out of your hair."

I can see Dad about to protest, ask them to stay a little bit, but Hunter jets off to grab Jessica and in ten seconds flat, they've disappeared back through the gate as if they were never here.

"Weird guy," Harley says softly.

"What was that all about?" I ask as Amy takes her seat again.

She flushes. "Nothing really."

We all look at each other.

"That's not suspicious..." Kira says.

"Someone has a crush..." I tease.

Amy gasps. "Him?! No way. I have way higher standards than Hunter Ricks."

"Dang, tell us how you really feel," Harley says.

Amy huffs, her breath catching a curl of her hair in frustration. "Just because he's a dad doesn't mean he's not a playboy. Besides, he's way too cocky for me."

"Then what was that conversation about?" Dad asks, gesturing to the table. "We're all on the edge of our seats!"

"Well, he just–he was asking if he could have a copy of

my new book. Early. For Jessica. That's it," Amy explains and then starts poking at some eggs on her plate.

We all watch her, wanting more information. But it never comes.

"So. DJ or live band?" Amy asks, effectively moving on from the conversation.

Something tells me there's more to that story. Although, that's every story in the Solace family. Everyone always knows a little more than they're letting on. Including me. I'm not exempt. The trick, though, is not letting anyone in on my secrets. That way, I never have anyone meddling in my business.

Except the universe knows what's going on beneath the surface. And the universe loves to throw me curveballs.

12

AXEL

I try to go about my Saturday as usual. Hit the gym, grab a coffee, do work because who needs a weekend when you're a workaholic.

My mind, though, doesn't stop racing. Eventually, I'm just sitting at my computer staring at the screen, my heart throbbing with the thought that I'm one decision away from being disowned by my father.

So, I get up, grab my keys, and get back into my car. I drive for hours without knowing where I'm going. Part of that is just the evils of LA traffic. You try and go for a jaunt down the Pacific Coast Highway and suddenly you're held up in a line of cars fifty deep with motorcycles whizzing past you between lanes. The other part is knowing the decision I need to make in order to keep things the same versus the decision I want to make...which would mean everything changes.

I'm nowhere closer to deciding what to do.

On one hand, dating Linda Drosney, even if it's fake, for just a few months, wouldn't be so bad. I mean, who is to say she'd even want me longer than a couple of dates. Hell, her children could come between us. After all, if I was her son, I wouldn't be comfortable with her new boyfriend not being even a decade older than me.

On the other...it feels so wrong. I can feel it in my gut. And I'm not that type of person. I'm not like...well, I'm not like Gillian. I don't believe in the power of impulses or the universe guiding me with a kind hand or whatever the fuck. I have always dealt with facts, figures, and plots of land.

Not feelings.

It's partway through the yammering in my head that I realize what I need most. Peace and quiet. Rare to find that in LA. But I know a place.

I follow the PCT down its aching winds until I've finally lost the hordes of traffic. The sun is just starting to lower, sending sprays of color through the sky. Perfect timing. Since it's spring, it's not quite as warm as the tourists would like it to be, so they're already clearing off the beach.

I get out of the car and open the trunk, ditching my leather shoes for canvas flipflops and pulling a thick sweatshirt over my button down. I always have stuff on hand for an impromptu walk through nature.

It was something I was able to do a lot more often when I wasn't a workaholic. Hiking, surfing, swimming. I miss that guy.

For now, though, I'll revisit him.

I start walking down the beach to my spot. Or should I say my mother's spot. There's a pocket of rocks that make it look like the beach has ended, especially at high tide. But if you catch it just right, you can sneak past in ankle deep water and find a perfect little cove, untouched by people, where you can sit and think.

I haven't been there in...a while. I told myself I didn't need it.

But that wasn't it.

I just couldn't stand to be reminded of her.

The tide is halfway when I make it to the rocky outcrop. I pull up the front of my pants and wade through the water. It sloshes around my calves.

I take a deep breath as I round the corner, ready to feel my mother's presence.

However, I am thrown completely off-balance when I see someone is already sitting on my private beach.

The last person I'd like to see.

"Gillian," I say, my mouth already starting to go dry. "What are you doing here?"

Gillian looks up and gets to her knees. "Oh my god, sorry, I didn't know you'd–" She picks up the blanket she was sitting on. "I'll go, I'll–"

"No, no. It's fine, you don't have to go." My stomach knots as I remember the last time the two of us were here together. I had brought her here to show her the spot. My secret spot. And we'd...It's not worth thinking about it. That's so far away. "I mean. I'm not going to make you."

"If you want to be alone, I'll go. Really."

"It's okay." I take a few steps forward, my feet making deep imprints in the sand. "Actually, can I join you?"

Gillian considers my question for a moment. I think if we were anywhere else in the world, she'd tell me to eat dirt. But she knows what this spot means to me. She wouldn't do that here.

Even at her worst, she's kind of the best.

"Yeah. Sure." She spreads out the blanket again. I help her straighten out the edges. Then, the two of us sit down and fall into silence as we look out at the water.

"I, uh...didn't know you still came out here," I say softly.

I notice Gillian flush out of the corner of my eye. "Um. Well, yeah. It's a good spot. To clear your head."

"Do you come here a lot?"

She looks at me bashfully and nods. But then she quickly shakes her head. "I mean. You know, when I can. Which isn't that often, I guess. The bakery and Stella take up most of my time. Wish I could get out here more, honestly."

"Where's Stella now?"

"She's...with my dad. Maybe I'm a bad mom, but I just needed some time to myself."

I smile solemnly. "Gillian, you're definitely not a bad mom. Everyone needs a moment alone sometimes."

She sighs. I can tell she doesn't believe a word I've said. I don't blame her. "Anyway, what are you doing here?"

"Well, *my* dad is being a pain in my ass."

"As usual," she says.

I laugh loudly.

"Sorry, I shouldn't have said that."

"No, you're right. He's being his usual, awful self."

Gillian tilts her head to the side. Her long blonde hair looking even more like gold in the halo of sunset. "You want to talk about it?"

I groan. "There's not much to say. Besides it has to do with, you know, the thing that has to do with you."

"Oh," she says with a small chuckle. "Well, I think here we can put our differences aside."

I glance around the cove. This was our spot seven years ago. This is where we could come and be truly alone, untouched by anyone else. We didn't have to feel the guilt of getting closer to one another. It was our own private hamlet of where we could explore each other's bodies, laugh as loudly as we wanted, and just *be* together. No threat of being found out. No worrying about Lola returning from her summer abroad. Just Gillian and me. "Okay. If you're sure."

Gillian nods. "I am."

I take a deep breath. "Well, basically, I don't know if you saw that photo in the Times this morning, but I went to this gala a couple days ago and–"

"Oh, I saw," she says dryly.

I eye her, unsure of her meaning, but go on. "Basically, some cougar was coming onto me, and I couldn't get rid of her. Come to find out she's on the city council. And my dad wants me to date her to make sure the plans go through for the development."

Gillian gasps and then bursts into laughter.

"I know, it's hilarious."

"No, it's just–" She hides her face in her hands. " I saw the photo and assumed that was your new girlfriend or something."

I gape at her. "Girlfriend? Her?! No way. She's like fifteen years older than me. At least!"

"I only saw her from the back! How was I supposed to know?"

I start laughing too. "No way, Gill. Besides, when have I ever had a girlfriend?"

Her laughter dies out like an ember in a fire; she pulls her legs up to put her chin on one knee. "That's true. You've never been the girlfriend type."

Never have been. Ever. But that doesn't mean I couldn't be. Maybe someday, right? I don't blame her if that's impossible to see.

"Gillian..."

She stares out at the water. "What, Axel?"

Seven years is a long time. It should be enough time to forget. But I never have. Not the way her body felt in mine, not the way she made my heart skip a beat, not the way I wished it could last forever. "I'm sorry."

Gillian's body goes rigid.

"For...how it went down, you know? I wasn't as mature as I should have been and—"

"It's okay. That was a long time ago."

I stare at her, begging her silently to look at me. But her eyes won't move from the horizon. "It's not okay. I was a jerk."

"Yeah, you were, but it's okay. Really."

"Gillian—"

"Axel, it's not worth talking about again, okay?"

I screw my lips shut. Best not to push it any further than I already have. But I got to apologize. That's more than we've spoken about our summer fling in seven years. Not too shabby, I guess.

"I'm sorry too," she says softly. "We never should have crossed that line."

That's honestly not what I wanted her to say. I don't want her to regret it. How could she not, though, when our relationship has gone from bad to worse all this time?

"Less so because of Lola, but because I lost a really great friend," Gillian says, forcing a smile.

I nod. "Yeah. We were pretty close, weren't we?"

"Yeah. I sometimes think about all the things we've missed out on because we fucked it all up and slept together. All the memories we could have had."

So many memories...

"Anyway. I'm feeling nostalgic cause of all this, I guess," she says, waving her hands toward the cove.

"Me too."

Although my version of nostalgia is coming with an intense pull in my gut, a feeling that makes me want to reach out and kiss her, remember exactly how it felt when we belonged to each other.

That'd be crazy, wouldn't it?

13

____

GILLIAN

GOD, I WISH HE WOULD JUST LEAN OVER AND KISS ME.

Stop me from saying anything else stupid. Or keep me from feeling like I have to say anything at all.

Because I'd really like to tell him the truth. About Stella.

That's why I'm out here, actually. Why I left her with my dad for a couple hours, so I could just clear my head and think.

After Hunter Ricks left with Jessica and all us girls were cleaning up after brunch, Stella stopped and stood still for a while, her face quizzically screwed together.

"What is it, babe?" I asked her, not thinking anything of it.

"Jessica doesn't have a mommy."

I don't have the full story on that. I don't think her mom is entirely out of the picture, but clearly, she isn't much in it either.

"And I don't have a daddy."

I stopped in my tracks with whatever I was doing.

"That's not true, honey. You have a daddy. And Jessica has a mommy, they just—"

Stella crossed her arms over her chest. "They just don't want us."

I have never said that to her. Ever. "Who told you that?"

She lifted her chin obstinately. She wasn't going to tell me.

"That's not...true, honey."

"Then where is my daddy?"

I swallowed. This has become more and more of a problem lately. She wants to know so badly it's becoming a need. And who can blame her? She's six years old. All she's ever known is my sisters, her grandfather, and me. "Stella, I told you, it's a little complicated to—"

"Well, then maybe Jessica and I could trade."

I couldn't believe what I was hearing. "What?"

"Maybe she could have you for a week. And I could have her daddy for a week. And then we'll both know what it's like to have a mommy and a daddy."

It broke my heart. For so many reasons. One, that she had rationalized it in her head that way, that somehow, she can get that thing she so desperately wants if she just tinkers with the system. Two, that she might want to trade me in. She didn't say it like that, but how else am I supposed to take it? I've never been enough for her. And I've been a fool to think I ever was.

And three. Three is the hardest one.

That despite wanting to tell her with every fiber of my soul, I can't. Because her father doesn't even know he's her father.

I pawned Stella off on my dad (a job he's always more than happy to have) and rushed out here.

I've been coming to the cove ever since Axel showed it to me seven years ago. Never have I run into him since.

Now, by some hideous stroke of fate, he's sitting next to me. Stella's father, Axel Hitchins.

I've never had the strength to tell him. Never thought he really deserved it, honestly, after the way everything shook out.

But now, in this place we called our own seven years ago, I want to tell him. I want to tell him so bad. Then maybe I can give Stella what she's always wanted and what she deserves more than anything.

"Maybe we can call a truce, huh?" Axel says, interrupting the silence left by my pause to think.

"A truce..."

"That we can put everything behind us and be friends again."

Bringing up his paternal right to Stella would be the exact opposite of putting everything behind us. And I'm so eager to have that relationship with Axel again that I'm not sure I want to spoil it with a bombshell like that.

Stella will have to wait another day. "Okay...what does that entail?"

"Well, no more slander in the media."

"I haven't been slandering you."

Axel smiles cheekily. I want to slap that smile off his face with my lips. "No more interviews, then. No more interfering. The council will decide what it decides and we'll both back off whatever the answer is. How does that sound?"

I consider. It sounds...bad. But to have Axel back in any capacity that doesn't involve us always at odds with each other sounds *perfect*. "Okay. Deal."

"Wow, that's it? No negotiating."

I sigh, shaking my head. "I am so tired of negotiating, Axel."

"You taking up law, Gillian?"

I scoff. "No, can you imagine? No, it's more like negotiating bedtime, negotiating dessert, negotiating screen time."

"Is Stella a tough customer?"

If only he knew how much she was like him. He would be eating his words because he would *know* just how stubborn she was. I didn't know hardheadedness was a hereditary trait, and yet here I am. "Tougher than you, Axel." '

"Oooh. Bet. I'd like to see it."

I'd like that too. "Well, maybe someday soon. We'll just have to see."

"Guess so." Axel's eyes have never looked more green than right now. I'm trying not to match them with Stella's in my mind, but I can't help it. Her eyes are an exact copy of his. He holds out a long, pale hand. "Shake on it?"

I take his hand. "Shake on it."

This isn't a shake like people making a business deal, though. This is just our hands folding together. Squeezing tight. All my nerves and synapses are remembering his touch once again.

We can't keep doing this.

Or else I might just die.

"You've got a grip like a man," he mumbles.

I gasp. "I do not!"

"Yeah, you do. Have you taken up wrestling or something? Your strength is brutal, Gillian."

I jerk his hand closer to me; Axel winces. "That's what you get for testing my strength."

"Damn! Okay, I get it. You're strong. What do you want, an award?"

I relax my hold on his hand, so we are just sitting palm

to palm again. I look down at our hands, watch as his thumb traces back and forth over my skin. Yeah, this is real "just friends" territory, isn't it?

Well, it has to be. Until I'm told otherwise. And Lola miraculously changes her mind on the whole "don't date my brother" thing.

"Gill."

I lift my eyes to his. God, he's way too close. I can smell his cologne. Much more grown up than he used to be. Intoxicating. Makes me ravenous for his lips. For everything.

No. If he's not going to stop it, I will. Right fucking now.

I pull my hand away and put it sternly between my knees. "Well, anyway. That will certainly save everyone a lot of heartache, huh?"

"Y-yeah...Lola will be thrilled to know we've given up the ghost."

Silence washes over us once more, just like the tide lapping at the shore. Each moment, the world gets darker, the sun sinking lower.

And just like that, another opportunity to let Axel Hitchins know what he really means to me slips out of reach.

14

AXEL

A couple weeks have gone by as easy as breathing. We await the city council's decision with bated breath, but everything has changed.

Mostly because, though Gillian and I are on opposite sides of this issue, things don't feel like they're on fire anymore. I've managed to quell Dad's temper (although I think I owe most of that to Lola...she's a saint for putting up with him) and now that the lot and our plans for development isn't on the nightly news, I think he's off my back for the time being.

At the end of the day, Gillian and I are friends. If we are well and truly able to come back from a seven-year hiatus after one steamy summer, then we certainly can make it through whatever drama comes with the Seton lot.

However there's one thing I can't really ignore.

There's still that spark there.

Between Gillian and me.

I remember the very first time I felt it. I was sixteen and Gillian had skinned her knee while she and Lola were rollerblading. I was at home minding my own business when they burst inside, tears streaming down both their faces because Gillian was in pain and, to this day, Lola can't stand the sight of blood.

So, I had to be the big brother and take care of it.

Gillian and I were curled up in the downstairs bathroom, her sitting on the edge of the sink and me pasting a big bandage to her knee.

I remember the moment so clearly when she reached down and touched the back of my hand. "Thanks, Axel."

God, we were just kids. It wasn't a sexual feeling. But I felt something. Like we were kindred spirits or...soul bonded.

I don't know. I think Gillian is rubbing off on me a little too much, all her granola, hippy slang.

That feeling has been there a long time. I thought maybe we had gotten it out of our system seven years ago.

But when I saw her at the cove again, that idea went right out the window.

The spark. Haven't forgotten about it since.

I'm thinking about it right now as I lay in bed a whole hour before my alarm is supposed to go off.

What if I had just gone for it? Reached out and kissed her? I mean, the feeling was there, wasn't it?

I reach down under the sheets and grab my half-hard dick. The second I touch it, it bursts to life. Ready to attend to my every need of arousal.

I'm only halfway sorry to admit this is not the first time I've touched myself to the memory of Gillian and me at the cove.

I've mapped it out perfectly in my head to create pique arousal.

Instead of letting her pull her hand away, I tighten my grip and whisper, "Don't go."

Her brown eyes widen. Not with fear. With curiosity.

And I just lean in and I do it. I kiss her. Her body melts into mine without a second thought. In my fantasy, we both want this so bad that there's no question that we have to do it right here, right now. I wish that was the case in reality too.

Gillian breaks away and buries her face in my neck, "Axel..."

"Yes?"

"I can't stop thinking about you."

Just a little bit of confirmation to let me know I'm not fucking crazy. "I think about you all the time, Gill."

I can feel her smile on my neck. You know you have it bad for a girl when just the feeling of her smile makes your cock jump.

I press my face into her cheek and sigh. "Gillian, let me take care of you. Let me make love to you."

In all the times our bodies have compressed, it has never been lovemaking. It has been feverish and sweltering, angry and aggressive, silly and laugh-filled.

But love? That's something we have never touched. I'm not sure if that's a word I should use for her. We're just friends, after all.

This is my fantasy, though, right? I can just go with it.

Gillian sighs and nods, dreamy eyes. She pulls away and spreads her arms. "Take me."

Now this is where my imagination gets mushy. All the removal of clothing can be so awkward and silly in real life. But this is my imagination and it's supposed to feel like a movie, so in my head the clothing just tumbles off and then we're both naked on the beach, laying on her little blanket.

I've got her pinned underneath me. It's like *From Here To Eternity* except less war.

And her body is so warm, yet pricked with goosebumps.

"Did you miss me?" she asks softly as she guides my hands up from her hip to her breasts, bending my fingers around the plump flesh. "Did you think about me?"

I cannot lie. "Yes."

"How much?"

I sigh. "All the time."

Our lips find one another's again and because it's a fantasy, somehow our pelvises just lock into place, my cock slipping inside her tight, warm pussy.

This is when reality always comes washing over me again because my hand starts moving faster around my dick and I start getting worried I'll come too fast. That's how vivid this fantasy is.

We lay on our sides, bodies interlocking. I slide in and out of her, bare, watching the place our hips meet over and over. Gillian makes the most beautiful sounds, whimpering and clinging to me. She's missed me. She doesn't have to say it with words, I can feel it. Just the way her muscles are curling with pleasure.

The sounds of the beach swirl around us. Birds cawing, water lapping at the shore, an easy sea breeze.

Beach sex is much messier in real life. I know this from the time Gillian and I did it. Sand gets everywhere. It's...ridiculous.

Which is why fantasies are so great. No sand anywhere. Just ecstasy.

Because that's what Gillian is. Her body. The feeling of her skin. It should be illegal that it feels so amazing.

And of course, her perfect pink center, the one I'd like to burrow inside until the day I die.

"I need you. I need you so bad," she pants.

And inside, I know just what she means.

"Come inside."

This is when it gets really dicey. My hand isn't even fast enough. I have to push myself up into my hand as if I'm fucking her for real.

"Come inside me and claim me, Axel."

My brain starts to flood with a million questions. Is it just inherently arousing, the thought of coming inside someone and leaving my seed to grow? Or is that what I really want? Want not just the experience of becoming a part of someone but the whole journey after that too?

Do I want to be that deeply enmeshed?

Gillian then starts to moan in my little fantasy, her breath quickening, her nails digging into my skin. I can feel her desperation through her hips. They seize against me over and over. Our hips bump into each other, the rush of pleasure building and building and –

"Axel, give me *everything*."

"Shit, fuck, ah–" I choke out in pleasure from just touching myself to the thought of her.

Come spews up onto my belly and sits there, aching for a place to call home.

"Sorry, guys," I mutter when I recover enough. "Maybe next time."

Although the next time my cock finds a home, I'm pretty sure it won't be Gillian. She won't let me touch her with a ten-foot pole. That handshake, the one I've been living off of, was already crossing a line.

As much as I want her, I think I need to give up on the idea of her.

That's way easier said than done.

I PULL up in front of the bakery and put my car in park.

I just don't know what's good for me, do I? To be fair, I came to see Lola.

At least, that's what I'm telling myself.

I don't know if I'm going to even get my foot in the door seeing as the store is currently swarmed with cyclists. There are piles of bikes out front and cyclists littering all the picnic tables, a line of them trailing out the door. What the hell is going on?

"Excuse me," I cry out. I get a few nasty glares, but I'm not trying to cut the line. Just trying to see what the hell is going on.

When I finally get in the front door, I see Lola working like a madwoman behind the counter.

"Lola!"

She looks up, her eyes frazzled.

"What's going on?" I cry out.

She's about to answer, but her attention is taken away by a biker dressed in neon yellow towering over the shop.

"Cycling club."

I look over at the source of the voice. Little Amy Solace. Well, not so little anymore. Always little in my eyes. She's sitting at one of the café tables, accompanied by Stella. "Cycling club?"

"Apparently, they made this their twenty-mile marker. Guess even cyclists can't say no to sweet treats," Amy says with a shrug.

"Yeah, guess not."

"Hi, Axel!" Stella pipes up.

I smile. "Hey, kiddo. Your mom around?"

Stella takes a deep breath to answer, but Amy cuts her off. "I was watching Stella while Gillian goes wedding dress shopping with Harley and was just dropping her off to hang out with Lola so I can make a meeting with my editor, but..." Amy glances back at Lola who is doing her best to be grace under fire.

"Well, you gotta go meet with your editor."

Amy glances at Stella who is working on a coloring page, so concentrated her tongue is curled outside her mouth. "I can't just leave Stella here. Not while Lola isn't focused."

"I'll be fine!" Stella chirps.

"*Stella.*"

"I can watch her," I say. *Me and my big mouth, always saying anything that comes to mind without actually thinking how it sounds or what it actually entails.*

Stella stops coloring and looks up at me with an eager smile.

"Uh, I don't know about that, Axel. You know with everything..." Amy says.

Guess Gillian hasn't relayed the memo that things are hunky dory between us. "Trust me, we'll be okay. You gotta get to your meeting, right?"

She chews on the inside of her cheek. "Are you sure?"

"Positive."

Amy looks at me and then at Stella. "Stella, honey, will you be–"

"Yep!" Stella answers without hearing the rest of the question.

"Uh, okay then. Well, that's promising." Amy bounces onto her feet and comes up to me, giving me a squeeze on the shoulder. "I owe you."

I shake my head. "What are friends for?" And I mean it. Plus, I kind of feel like I'm lucking out. I get to hang out with a pretty cool kid without her mom around. Kids are the coolest when they feel like they're getting away with stuff.

Amy flits out of the shop through the flurry of cyclists.

"Well? You just gonna stand there?" Stella asks brazenly before patting a chair beside her. "Sit a spell."

I chuckle as I sit. "You've certainly got spunk, kid."

"Mommy says I'm spunky a lot."

I watch as Stella goes back to her coloring. "Well, you take after her, then. Your mom is one of the spunkiest people I know."

Stella suddenly drops a crayon. "Are you and mommy friends now?"

My eyebrows jump. "Now?"

"Yeah, because you want to get rid of the play lot and Mommy doesn't want you to."

Open communication. Makes sense for Gillian. When I was a kid, my parents talked about everything serious behind closed doors. Now, here we are, just talking about our issues in the open.

"And I don't want you to, either!" Stella warns, wagging a crayon at me.

"Duly noted," I say. "I'll tell my dad." I'm not sure the words of a six-year-old would make him change his mind any, but hey, couldn't hurt to try.

"Your dad?!"

I half-laugh. "My dad and I work together."

"Wow. That's cool."

Not as cool as you might think, kiddo. "It's hard sometimes. Do you and your mom ever argue?"

"Not argue. We disagree. That's what Mommy calls it."

"Hm. Well, my dad and I disagree. A lot."

Stella laughs and sinks down into her chair, looking off for a moment. "I guess I just think it's cool you have a dad."

Shit. Didn't even think about that... "You have a pretty cool Grandpa."

"Yeah, but Grandpa is Mommy's dad. Not *my* dad."

"No. I guess you're right..."

Stella goes back to coloring. I'm not sure what to say next. I look around the shop at the waning line of cyclists and then back to Lola at the counter. Though she's still fielding orders, she takes a moment to look at me and give me an encouraging thumbs up.

I glance back at Stella. "So, what do you need me to do here?"

"See all the leaves?" she asks, gesturing to the jungle scene on her paper.

"Yeah?"

Stella reaches into her crayon box and pulls out the nub of what was once a long green crayon. "They're your job."

I take the crayon. "You got it, boss."

15

_____

GILLIAN

"Hate it. Too floofy." Harley shimmies back and forth in the mirror, watching the dress slosh around. "It's a courthouse wedding, not *Bridgerton*."

The bridal consultant, a dark-haired woman with rosy cheeks and big black rimmed glasses grimaces. "Got it."

I laugh to myself. That's just Harley. Brutally honest. I've known her since she was born and I know not to take it personally. But not everyone can recognize that right off the bat.

"I think you look beautiful," Dana coos, circling Harley on the pedestal. "I mean, you look like a princess."

"Barf," Harley says.

Dana narrows her eyes. "Don't 'barf' at that."

"I'll barf at what I want to barf at."

"Can we not talk about barf?" I say.

Harley rolls her eyes. "It's not right. And I look fat."

Not this again.

"I want to try the black," Harley says, stomping her feet.

"You can't wear black," Dana repeats for the five hundredth time.

"It's my wedding, Dana!"

"Right. *Wedding.* Not a funeral. Tell her, Gillian."

I look at Harley apologetically. She knows I can't fight this battle. Dana only ever wants for us to be happy. When she holds an opinion staunch, you know you're not getting her to budge on it.

Harley's face tightens in aggravation. "Could you give us a minute?" she asks the consultant.

"No problem." She disappears without a second thought.

"What's your problem, Dana?"

Dana opens her mouth and then closes it.

"You're acting like this is your wedding."

"I'm not acting like that," our eldest sister says in an admonishing tone.

"You are!"

"Gillian," Dana looks my way. "Am I acting like this is my wedding?"

I look between my two sisters on opposite sides of a match as tense as Wimbledon. "Um..."

"That's a yes," Harley interrupts.

"No, I just think..."

Dana stomps over to the rack of dresses we picked out earlier. "There's gotta be another one here."

"There is! It's black!" Harley says edgily.

"Guys, can we just cool it for a second?" I say. "This is supposed to be a special day, right?"

Dana and Harley are quiet as they look at me.

"Let's just...try the black dress."

Dana starts to protest.

"And then, if we hate it, we can tell her! Harley loves an honest opinion."

Her lip curls up. "Well, I used to. But ever since I became a mom…"

"Oh, shut up and try the dress on."

Harley takes the dress and disappears into the back to find the consultant again, leaving Dana and I alone. Quiet.

"I wish you wouldn't have done that," Dana says.

I roll my eyes. "Why?"

"Because it's her wedding. It's bad enough she just want us to get it over with at the courthouse, but now you're saying she can wear *black*?"

"Dana, since when did you have a problem with her getting married at the courthouse?"

My older sister huffs and crosses to a rack of dresses we've perused many times and determined were too glittery for Harley's taste. She rifles through them like someone opening the fridge ten minutes after checking it the first time. "It's just supposed to be the best day of her life, you know?"

"You sound like Mom."

Dana stops and glares at me.

"Not in a bad way!"

She goes back to shuffling through the dresses. "Someone has to sound like Mom around here."

I smile sadly. "Is that what this is about? Making sure you're like Mom?"

It's a complicated balance to strike when you have a mother who betrayed you. Mom walked out on us a little over ten years ago. Sure, she reared her head back into our lives last year, but it wasn't genuine. It wasn't real. We all have to nurse that wound, carry the chips on our shoulders.

But she was also our mom. And we have so many fond memories of her. Not a day goes by where I don't hear her remind me of something in the back of my head.

Dana, the first born, has definitely been cursed to carry the heaviest of this burden.

"Hey, talk to me," I say softly and sidle up to her. I can see tears forming in her eyes.

"Someone has to make sure there are no regrets, you know? This is Harley's big day. It's–it's our *first* big day. And I don't want her to look back and regret not doing the big wedding or wearing the white dress or –"

"Not doing it *her* way?"

Dana zips her lips together and looks down. "Well, when you put it like that..."

"Listen, Dana, we're not here to keep her in check. We're just here to make her day special."

"I'm trying to." A tear slips down her face. "It's a lot of pressure to be–"

Fill in the blank. The eldest? The mom? "I know, Dana. But all Harley needs from you being here is *you* being here. Not who you think you're supposed to be."

Dana hums thoughtfully. "Wow, you should think about going into therapy or something, because that was pretty darn good, Gillian."

I giggle. "Only where my sisters are concerned." Because when it comes to my own life, I definitely don't know how to follow my own advice.

I give Dana a hug and she sighs. "Thank you."

"Any time."

"It's a little weird too that it's Harley first, don't you think?" Dana whispers. "I mean, just of all five of us, the rebel is getting hitched first?"

I try not to think about it, but yeah, it sits funny on my mind a lot. Especially because Harley and I had similar trajectories at least for a moment. Clandestine affairs, accidental babies...she just got the man too.

I try to be happy for her. I *am* happy for her. However, that doesn't mean it's not hard or that I don't think about an alternate timeline where I got up the courage to tell Axel the truth and that he embraced me and our baby wholeheartedly. Now, who knows what our lives would look like?

"You guys! This is it!"

Dana and I both turn to find Harley ascending the pedestal in a tea-length, black dress with a deep V in the front. So utterly simple and yet...

"Oh, Harley," Dana starts first, going toward our sister. "It's stunning."

"Are you crying, Dana?" Harley asks in shock.

I follow. "It's perfect." It really is. Quintessential Harley, not doing anything by the rules, marching to the beat of her own drum. Tana is a lucky little girl to have such a strong woman for a mother. I know Harley would say the same of Stella.

I hope she's right.

Dana and I huddle around Harley, tears springing to both our eyes. The consultant asks with delight, "Is this it?"

Harley wraps her arms around our shoulders. "Is it that obvious?"

It's moments like these that make me realize we can have a beautiful life without Mom. Scratch that. We *have* a beautiful life without Mom. It aches differently than a normal life. But damn does it *soar* sometimes.

16

AXEL

"You're doing a nice job staying in the lines," I say as Stella works on a very detailed butterfly.

"Thank you. Mommy says I don't have to stay in the lines, but that's why the lines are there," she replies, concentrating hard on being very careful.

"Your mom would say that," I say with a chuckle.

Stella stops and looks at my work on the leaves. "You do a nice job staying in the lines too."

"Yeah, well, like you said. They're there for a reason."

Stella smiles. "Exactly."

We continue to color in a comfortable silence.

"Everything okay over there?" Lola asks, wiping her hands on her apron.

The bakery has mostly cleared out now, all the cyclists sitting outside enjoying their cups of coffee and pastries.

"Peachy," I say. "You?"

"Well, that was a marathon."

"More like a triathlon," I reply.

Lola rolls her eyes. "*Stupid.*"

"What's a triathlon?" Stella asks, raising her eyes to meet mine.

For some reason, I get a little nervous. I'm not around kids very much and if I am, they're more ornamental in nature. What if I can't explain things in terms she can understand? "Well, you know what a marathon is?"

Stella nods. "Like a really long race."

"Yes, a running race. But in a Triathlon, you don't just run. You also ride on a bicycle."

Her eyes widen. "Whoa."

"And you swim too, but that's beside the point. Doesn't fit into—my joke was—"

"Axel was just being a smart aleck," Lola explains. "You know what that is, don't you, Stella?"

The little girl huffs. "I am not a smart aleck."

"Not all the time," Lola mutters.

I give Stella a playful nudge on the shoulder. "Hey, it's not so bad knowing everything. Sometimes people don't appreciate us."

Her eyes brighten. Sparkly green. Never noticed just how green they are.

Lola clears her throat. "Anyway, you want me to..." Her eyebrows lift. "...take over?"

I glance down at Stella and then back to Lola. "I think we're good. You take a break. You were just working your butt off."

Stella lowers her head and laughs. "Hehe...butt."

"Did I say something funny?" I tease.

"No..." she replies, lowering her head further down and then whispering, "*Butt.*"

I laugh. "I heard that!"

"Okay, well, as long as you're sure..." Lola continues

with a look that is asking me, *"Are you sure you can handle it?"*

"I think we're fine. What do you think, Stella?"

Stella smiles at Lola. "I'm fine, Auntie Lola."

Lola gives the little girl a smile. "Okay. If you need anything, I'll be in the office sipping coffee. Just a couple minutes."

"Take as many minutes as you want," I say.

"As many minutes as you *need*," Stella adds.

Lola giggles to herself. "You two are trouble, I can tell."

Stella and I exchange a brief look. I can't hold it for too long. I almost feel shy. Something about this little girl is so charming. So terribly familiar. A piece of Gillian and yet... feels like there's a little mystery to her I'm just starting to understand.

Lola disappears into the back with a cup of coffee and a long sigh, leaving Stella and me again to our quiet coloring.

"So, do you like to do anything else besides coloring?"

"Lots of things."

"You like to roller skate. I remember that one."

"Mhm."

"What else?"

She furrows her brow, concentrating. "I like to...play Legos."

"Good choice."

"And I like to read about aminals."

Aminals....that's fucking precious.

"An-i-mals," she corrects herself and then shakes her head. "I like to pretend to play an-i-mals with my friends."

"An-i-mals," I repeat.

"Don't make fun of me!"

"I'm not! Promise. It was just charming. You know, when I was your age, I couldn't pronounce my r's."

Stella stops coloring and looks at me. "Like how?"

"Like kind of like how British people don't pronounce their r's. Except I didn't have the rest of the British accent. And it didn't just happen at the ends of words, but at the beginnings too." I clear my throat. "Awound the wugged wocks the wugged wascal wan."

"Oh! There's a kid in my class who does that. Henry."

"I hope you're nice to him."

She gets a very serious expression. "Oh, I am. Promise. With a capital 'p'. That means I really mean it."

"Who taught you that one? I like it."

"Mommy."

"Ah. Mommy. Should have known," I say. I wonder what the two of them are like behind closed doors. Their special bond seems so magical. "Anyway, it's good that you're nice to him. Because kids weren't very nice to me about it."

Stella reaches out and touches my arm. "I'm sorry."

"Oh, it's okay. It's..." I look down at her little hand in the crook of my elbow. Damn. Maybe I'm not just a horned-up dude who has a breeding kink. Maybe the idea of having a little one of my own to protect and nurture is starting to hit me. Although they'd have to be as well-behaved and thoughtful as Stella. And kids are like rolling dice with millions of sides. You really never know what you're going to get. "I went to speech therapy. A nice lady helped me, so now I don't talk like that."

"But it's okay that you talked like that."

I nod. "Maybe. Kids can be mean sometimes."

Stella retracts her hand and looks away. "Yeah. They can."

There seems to be something she's not saying. "Are kids ever mean to you?"

She shrugs. "Sometimes. Mommy tells me not to listen to them because they're..." Stella looks side to side, "i-d-i-o-t-s."

"Your mother does not use that word."

"Yes, she does! Honest!"

Huh. Okay, then. "What are they mean to you about?"

Stella picks up a red crayon and starts to color in the head of a parrot. "They just ask a lot of questions."

"Like..."

"Like why I don't have a dad."

Nice, Axel. You just made a six-year-old talk about her trauma. Add that to the list of reasons you're going to hell. "Well, you have a dad, he's just..." Where *is* he?

I can't lie, the timing has always made me a little uneasy. However, the whispers from Lola and the Solace girls were that Stella belonged to Gillian's ex-boyfriend at the time, Martin. Gillian just didn't want to talk about it. I put any worries to bed very quickly after that.

"We don't need to talk about it," Stella says softly as if she's comforting me. "Mommy says it's none of their business and that plenty of kids only have a mommy or a daddy."

I put down my crayon. "You're still allowed to have feelings about it."

"I guess."

"I suppose maybe it makes you sad sometimes."

Stella nods. "And a little mad."

"Yeah, I get that too." Poor little one. Doesn't know how complicated life gets. I don't know how things went down between Martin and Gillian. I imagine she must have told him about the baby. Is it better that Stella not know who he is or know that maybe he didn't want to be a part of her life? She's little, but she's getting smarter by the day. It's obviously not my place to have an opinion. I just...guess I have a soft spot for Stella. "That sounds complicated. Do you and Mommy talk about it?"

"Sometimes. Mommy doesn't really like talking about it."

I feel a crack form in my heart. I know that Stella is the best thing that's ever happened to Gillian. We might not have been friends for many years, but it's obvious. The way she came into her own and conquered the world with a baby on her hip. Now, her baby is growing up faster than she probably wants. I think she's done a great job. Parenting just comes with the assumed risk of fucking some things up. "Can I tell you a secret?"

A grin spreads across her face. "I love secrets."

"Me too." I lean in closer to her and look around as if this is a clandestine maneuver. "Us grown-ups...we like to pretend we know everything. But we really don't know anything. We're just trying our best to make it through the day with both our shoes on."

Stella gasps in laughter and touches her mouth. "I knew it!"

I laugh. If she saw through the guise of adulthood that likes to put smoke and mirrors over the complications of life, then she's the smartest kid I've ever met.

Lola comes back out, her hair now pulled back into a nice ponytail, all the anxiety of the previous twenty minutes completely dissipated. She gives me a look to say, *"You good?"*

I give her a quick nod and a wink. I think things are better than good out here, actually.

Stella leans over on my knee to look at the page I've been coloring. She's just assumed a sort of closeness with me. And it doesn't feel weird at all. It's kind of nice.

Gillian just brings people together, I guess.

"You missed a leaf right there." She points to a corner on the page.

"I wasn't done! How dare you!"

Stella laughs as I grab her and start to tickle her sides.

"Snickerdoodles?" Lola puts a plate of cookies down in front of us.

"My favorite!" I say, except mine isn't the only voice I hear. Stella and I have just said it simultaneously. "Your favorite?" I ask eagerly.

She nods.

"It can't be your favorite. It's mine!"

"You're so silly, Axel," Stella says, swiping a cookie off the plate.

"I guess," I grumble and grab my own cookie. "Thanks, Lola."

Lola sits on the other side of the table. "Of course. When two people are coloring as hard as you, a snack is definitely in order."

"Mmphank you, Auntwie Wowa," Stella says with a mouthful of cookie.

Lola grins. "You're welcome."

Stella and I munch for a bit. I notice the crumbs are piling up in her lap, so I grab a napkin from the holder on the table and set it down on her lap. Then, I brush her hair off her shoulders, so they don't act as crumb catchers. "There," I say softly.

I feel Lola's gaze harden on me. Being the only girl in the family, she can call attention without so much as saying a word if she stares at you hard enough. I look at her nervously. "What?"

"Nothing, it's just..." She shrugs. "You're kind of a natural."

I frown. "Huh?"

Lola gestures between Stella and me. "You're good with her."

"Well, she's good with me. Right, Stella? You put up with me just fine, huh?"

"Yeah!" Stella laughs.

Lola's demeanor remains tender. "Stella's good with everyone. Or she puts up with most everyone I should say." Then, her brow furrows. "But you...I don't know. I never knew you were good with kids, Axel."

I swallow a bite of cookie, hoping the gulp isn't terribly loud. If that isn't confirmation of what I've been wondering, I don't know what is. Like I said, Stella knows how to bring the best out in people. I don't know if she's real proof that I am any good with children.

However, hearing Lola say that...it ignites a want that's always been there in the background, smoldering as it waits to be acknowledged.

I've been pretending all these years that I'd be fine to live my life as a playboy. Working my ass off to keep growing the family business, not stopping to worry about the actual *family* aspect. What would be the point of living a life for a business when it can't love you back? It can't give you a hug or ask you about your day. Can't make you feel wanted or needed without also making you feel like you're just a part of the machine.

Before I can respond to Lola, Gillian walks through the front door.

In an instant, everything clicks into place.

My greatest goal in life is no longer power and success. It's love and family.

And I think I want it with Gillian.

17

GILLIAN

I know something is up when I see Axel's car parked outside the bakery. How is it that I leave for just a couple hours and somehow, he shows up out of the blue? This guy is *haunting* me.

As I walk up to the front door, I spy Axel through the window sitting next to Stella. My heart races. *What the fuck is he doing?*

They're smiling. Laughing. It triggers something inside me, an intense swell of emotion I don't know how to describe. All I know is I need to get Stella away from him because she is mine and I'm not going to let him hurt her too.

I rush inside, ignoring the chorus of hellos, and scoop Stella up into my arms, hugging her tightly. Axel is staring at me with confusion, and I suddenly realize that in my blind rage, I didn't even see Lola sitting at the table too.

I look like a freak.

"Hi baby..." I say breathlessly, trying to modulate the tension. "How was your day?"

"Mommy, you're squeezing too tight," Stella peeps.

I release my grip, but don't put her down. "Sorry, I just...missed you today."

Stella examines my face, green eyes probing my expression for the truth.

"What are..." I look at Axel. "What are you doing here?"

He swallows, his Adam's apple bobbing in his throat. "I was–"

"He was helping me out," Lola explains quickly. "Amy came by to drop Stella off, and we were absolutely swamped with cyclists."

I frown. "Cyclists?"

"They were using the bakery as a twenty-mile marker, so we were just swarmed. I couldn't step away and–"

"Amy had a meeting with her editor," Axel blurts. "And I offered to sit with Stella until Lola was finished up and then, you know, one thing led to another and–"

I shoot laser eyes at him. "One thing led to another" is an expression reserved for accidentally fucking his sister's best friend, not hanging out with my daughter.

Axel gets the hint. "We were having a nice time, that's all."

"Yeah, Mommy," Stella says adamantly. "We were coloring together."

My vision finally clears completely and I see the table littered with crumbs and crayons. Two plates with half-eaten cookies. In the center is Stella's big coloring book. "You two made a lot of headway on that one, huh?" I ask, cracking a smile even though I'm still on high alert.

"Yes, Axel is very good at coloring inside the lines," Stella says with a nod.

"Well. Great," I reply. What the hell else am I supposed to say when I tore in here like a bat out of hell and basically stared Axel down as if he was luring my daughter into an unmarked white van with candy? He was taking care of her. Watching her. But somehow that doesn't make me feel better at all. The longer he spends with her, the sooner I think he's going to see the truth. How can he not see it?

They have the exact same eyes.

"Everything's fine," Lola says softly, touching my back as she returns behind the counter with a skeptical look in her eye.

"Could you put me down, Mommy?" Stella asks. "I'm not done with my cookie."

"Oh, yes, sorry," I say and let Stella back down to the ground. I hadn't even noticed how my muscles were starting to ache from holding her, she's gotten so big.

"Axel's favorite cookie is a snickerdoodle too," she says before taking a big bite of her cookie.

I nod. "I knew that, actually." My eyes meet Axel's. Is he smiling? God, why did I say that? That brings back way too many memories. I perfected the recipe based on his tastebuds that summer seven years ago. He was my guinea pig. If it wasn't so popular among the customers, I'd throw the recipe right in the garbage and never make another snickerdoodle cookie again in my life.

"You want to sit, Gillian?" he asks, gesturing to the seat across from him.

I eye the chair carefully. "Uh. Yeah. Sure." Any other answer would just be taken as melodramatic, and I've already made things weird enough. I sit down across from them. We all remain silent as Stella finishes her cookie. Axel doesn't touch his again. I think I probably made him lose his appetite with that scathing eye contact I've been giving him.

"How was wedding dress shopping?" he asks suddenly.

I frown. "How do you know about that?"

"Amy told me," he says. "Your life isn't exactly classified, Gillian."

"Yeah, Mommy. It's not exactly *classified*," Stella repeats.

I gape at her. "Do you even know what that means?"

She shrugs. "No. I just wanted to say it."

Axel laughs. "You did a good job, kiddo."

My brain feels like it's burning. How dare he call her by a pet name? How dare he act like a fun uncle when that's not what he actually is to her? Not at all. I have to hold my tongue, but I'm so furious it's actually starting to hurt.

Because underneath all the fury and anger, I love it. I love it so much. It's all I've ever wanted for her. A male figure in her life... a father. My dad does his best, but he's her *grand*father and that's different. Especially now that she isn't the only grandchild. No, Stella needs a father of her own.

And even though Axel is technically that, it can't be him.

Can it?

"Classified basically means like secretive. You know how we were telling secrets earlier? Well, we can call those classified," Axel says, looking askance at me with a smirk.

"Secrets?" I ask. "What kind of secrets?"

Stella shrugs. "Sorry, Mommy. Classified."

"There ya go," Axel chuckles.

Don't you dare smile, Gillian. This isn't cute. It's annoying.

No. It's really cute. Although I'm terrified to think about what kind of secrets they were trading back and forth. Were they talking about me?

"Um, wedding dress shopping was good."

"Just good? Did you find '*the one*'?" Axel says with melodramatic flair.

I can't help but smile just a bit. "Yes, we found 'the one'."

"Ah...well, a shame Harley isn't having a real ceremony, so I won't be able to see her walk down the aisle. Or...does a courthouse have an aisle?" he asks with a cock of his eyebrow.

"I think so? I don't really know." I glance at Stella who has started coloring again. "You'll come to the party, though, won't you?"

Axel opens his mouth and carefully says, "I hadn't really considered it."

"Well, you're invited."

"Right, I wasn't sure if it was just a formality or..."

It's been a formality for every family event over the past seven years. At least for me. For all my sisters, Lola and Axel are a package deal. They're invited to everything. Lola always comes, Axel's attendance is usually a toss-up. He never stays for too long, though. Probably gets tired of my coldness. "You should come," I say.

Axel's eyes brighten.

"Harley would appreciate it," I say without looking at him. It's really me who would appreciate it.

"Well, I'll be there, then. For Harley's sake."

I can hear the subtext. He knows I don't actually mean that he should come because of Harley. He's just not willing to call me out. Which I appreciate.

Stella stops suddenly and slams down her crayon. "Mommy! What time is it?"

"Oh, yeah, we should probably get going," I say, checking my phone. "Yep, nearly one. We should head out."

"Where you off to?" Axel asks as Stella starts to collect

all the crayons, shoving them into the box haphazardly. "Whoa, whoa, whoa, slow down, kiddo. Don't want broken crayons. I'll help you."

Why does he have to be so good with her? So willing to be helpful, so patient. I don't know this version of Axel. How come it comes out with Stella? Maybe he's just a nice guy when it comes to kids, and I've never really seen it. Or maybe...

Maybe he knows. Or maybe he feels it subconsciously. This child is different.

"It's the big end of school picnic! You should come!" Stella grins.

My eyes widen. "Stella, I don't know if that's such a good idea."

Axel scoffs. "Why not?"

I cross my arms. "Well, for starters, it's being held at the Seton lot."

His humored expression immediately drops.

"And...it'd be kinda weird since Axel isn't a parent at the school." *At least not that he knows.* "And doesn't really know any of the kids–"

Stella gasps. "He knows *me*!"

"Right, well, what I mean is–"

"I want him to come. You haven't even asked him if he can come. Can you come?" Stella asks eagerly.

"Axel is a very busy man, Stella."

He shakes his head. "Today, I'm not."

I narrow my eyes. *Why is he making this so difficult?*

"Perfect! Then you can come!"

Axel looks at Stella, then at me, and then back to Stella. "I would love to, but it would be up to your mother. I might just get in the way."

Stella jumps out of her seat and grabs my hand. "Can he come? Please, Mommy?"

I open my mouth to respond, but quickly stop. Her little hand is softly stroking mine; her eyes are wide and pleading. It's so hard to say no to her. Ever. I feel like I've denied her so much in life. I've denied her a traditional life from the very beginning. To deny her anything else makes me feel so guilty.

But this is Axel. I'm trying to protect her. Not to mention him showing up to the Seton lot is like yelling "Fire!" in a crowded airport. Who knows what kind of chaos he would start by being there?

"Stella, it's okay. You two will have your fun and I'll see you another time, how about–" Axel starts to intercede.

"Fine, he can come," I say finally, although my voice is so quiet, I'm not sure he heard me.

Lola did. All the way from her spot behind the counter where she's brewing another container of coffee. She freezes and looks over her shoulder at me. *Are you crazy?* her eyes ask. After the way Axel and I have been at each other's throats the past four months, she's right to be concerned.

Little does she know, it's not about that. Not about that at all.

"You sure, Gill?" Axel asks me.

Gill. Just a diminutive of my name. Yet, for him to call me that in front of other people. In front of my daughter–

Our daughter.

"Yeah, I'm sure," I say. *Ignore it. Means nothing.*

Stella leaps up in celebration, kissing me on the cheek. "Yay! Thank you, Mommy!" Then she rushes over to Axel and grabs his hand. "Mommy made us a picnic basket with food and everything. She made pigs in a blanket. They're my favorite. Can we take your car? I like your car better than Mommy's. It's bigger!"

Axel shakes his head around like it's full of marbles. "Whoa, whoa, whoa! One thing at a time."

Stella drags him by the hand outside, but Axel doesn't seem to resist. I sigh in their wake and look back at Lola. She shakes her head. "You're crazy, Gillian."

"Me? Your brother is the crazy one. Why would he want to spend his Saturday with his worst nightmare and her daughter?"

Lola's face softens. She doesn't reply with words. Just shakes her head and smiles.

What the hell kind of response is that?

Stella waves through the window at me. "Come on, Mommy!" she calls out, voice muted by the glass.

It's just one afternoon. It will be fine. It might even be good.

Better not get ahead of myself with that one, though.

I head outside and grab the picnic basket out of my VW bug while Axel gets Stella settled in his car. She's right. His car is bigger. And the air conditioning probably works a hundred percent of the time instead of seventy percent. I pop the basket into the backseat beside her, climb into the passenger seat, and sigh.

"You have no idea how excited I am to see the famous Seton lot in action," Axel remarks just before turning on the car.

I look out the window and grimace. What the hell have I gotten myself into?

18

AXEL

When we arrive at the Seton lot, I immediately get it. Everything snaps into place. From the pictures, all I've ever seen is a dusty lot covered in weeds with rickety chain link fence on two sides. However, right now, it is *alive*.

Children run through the grass playing games of Red Rover and tag while parents are posted up with strollers and wagons, picnic blankets scattered across the ground. There's a table set up by the PTA that's making root beer floats and another booth with facepainting.

There are various banners left up from the last protests. "Save our park!" and "Seton lot belongs to us!" Phrases I would roll my eyes at before.

Now, though...it's clicking into place.

"You okay?" Gillian asks.

"Sorry?"

"You've got kind of a glazed-over look on your face," she says with a half-smile. "Too much stimuli?"

Yes, but not in the way she means it. I couldn't fathom until this moment why so many people cared to fight for a measly plot of land. Other than one kid sobbing about a skinned knee, I don't see one sour face in the whole place. Everyone is grinning ear to ear. It's almost unsettling. But then I remember that some people are just...happy.

That's not the world I tend to live in. Businesspeople are always disgruntled and if they're smiling it's because they're trying to get something from you.

These are just parents and kids and teachers, all of whom are happy to be there. Happy to be alive.

"There's a spot over here by Jacob, Mommy!" Stella cries out and rushes toward a blanket where a mother is slathering sunscreen onto her little boy.

"Uhm, okay!" Gillian cries out in a strained voice. Then she looks at me. "This is a trial by fire, Axel. You think I'm bad, but you haven't met Fran."

Fran...I know the name. "Shapiro?"

"Mhm."

Oh, shit. That's the lawyer that's been on our ass every step of the way. She's really not going to be happy to see me.

"Just be nice. She won't do anything in front of her kids. But she does hate your guts," Gillian says.

"I'm used to that," I reply.

She gapes. "I don't hate your guts."

"Hm. Likely story."

Gillian laughs. "You're ridiculous."

My heart flutters. I'll be as ridiculous as needed since it makes her happy. I'll do whatever makes her happy, really.

Stella is already talking with the little boy when we get over there. And Fran has her eyes squarely on me. "Well, well, well..."

"Fran, this is Axel."

"I'm familiar."

I hold out my hand. "Pleasure to meet you. Your emails are very well written."

Fran takes my hand, though she eyes me like a crocodile. "Thank you. Have yet to see an email from you, though."

The lawyers take care of everything. Me getting involved would be bad for business and she knows it. She's just trying to get under my skin. "Well, maybe some time soon."

"What are you doing here, Mr. Hitchins?"

"I invited him!" Stella announces. "Can we go play now?"

Fran swipes a bit more sunscreen on her son's face before nodding. "Go. But when it's time to eat, it's time to eat. No 'five more minutes', alright?"

Stella and the little boy run off together and join a game of...something. I'm not sure. It's just a bunch of kids holding their arms out like airplane wings.

Childhood is so funny.

"So, you wanted to see what the deal was with this place, huh?" Fran asks as Gillian and I set down our picnic blanket and settle in.

"Well, yeah, I've heard so much about it and it's good to know how the other half is living, don't you think?"

"I suppose," Fran says.

Gillian gives her a look. "He's just here as a friend. No work."

"Doubt that, but...alright."

"Promise, not looking to fight," I say. "It'll be like I'm not even here."

Gillian and Fran start to gab about something. I tune them out while I continue people watching. With each passing moment, my guilt seems to grow. I'd be getting rid of this? A space so alive and free? For what? Another fucking condo.

It'd be wrong.

I can't believe I'm saying that, but it'd be so wrong.

My eyes continue to gravitate toward Stella as she threads in and out of games with different groups of friends. She crabwalks, cartwheels, runs like the wind, all with a breathless smile on her face. It's a place where she can be free. Be herself.

And her mother...

I glance at Gillian. Her eyes flick to Stella from time to time, but she's mostly involved in conversation with Fran.

This is freedom for Gillian too. Where she can trust in a big city such as LA that her community will take care of her and her little girl.

It's all hitting me at once so hard I think I might need to lay down.

"Okay, I need to grab Jacob so he can eat or else his blood sugar is going to drop and he's going to be grumpy," Fran says, popping to her feet. "Jacob! Time to eat!"

"You want me to grab Stella?" I ask.

Gillian shakes her head. "She'll come along too."

We sit in silence as we watch Fran chase down the game and almost get bowled over by a clump of kids playing a game of Five Hundred. I laugh and, as my laughter fades out, I say what's been on my mind since I've arrived. "Okay, you win."

"Hm?"

I look at Gillian. Her warm brown eyes are waiting for me to go on. "You win. I get it. Why you're fighting for this place."

She smiles in surprise. "Well, that's something, I guess.

Too bad you're not on the city council. Then that'd actually mean something."

I shake my head. "We don't need city council."

Gillian starts to unload the picnic basket. "What are you talking about?"

"What if I was able to make this into a real park?"

She stops and looks at me. "Hitchins wants to make a park?"

"Well, not in so many words. It's just started dawning in on me, honestly, but being here..." I sigh. "You're right. It would be a tragedy to get rid of it."

Gillian frowns. "Are you okay? Did you hit your head earlier today?"

I consider her for a moment. The breeze tousles her dirty blonde hair. Of course she has no reason to believe me. After everything. But I want her to. Desperately. "No, I think I've just gotten some clarity."

Her frown relaxes.

"We could have a jungle gym over here and have an open field over there. Entertainment for the kids, but still give space for communal events. And then we could–"

"Swings," Gillian interrupts. "We need swings."

I smile. "Yes, a park without swings would be nothing."

"And a bathroom. We need a bathroom."

"Of course."

"Water fountains."

I grin. "You've thought a lot about this."

Gillian flushes. "Of course I have."

What am I supposed to do with myself when she's so fucking adorable?

Her excitement fades. "How does that make you money? It's just a park."

It hurts, but it's fair. I've never given Gillian any reason to believe I care about anything but money and the bottom line. Mostly because up until very recently that *was* all I cared about. She doesn't know something is shifting deep inside me. Something I just don't know how to say aloud yet. "It doesn't," I say. "I'd need donors. But it's the right thing to do."

Gillian smiles at me. Not a forced smile. Not because she's laughing at a joke. A real, "I'm giving you a smile" smile.

The only way I want it to fade is if I kiss her.

Stella barrels over before I can do anything so foolish. "Food time!"

"First, hand sanitizer time!" Gillian announces, pulling out a bottle of sanitizer from her purse.

Gillian has packed an amazing spread in her picnic basket. There are pigs in a blanket for Stella and freshly made falafel, hummus, and veggie slices for us. Not to mention potato salad and chips, plus loads of fresh fruit. Even though it's mostly vegan, I'm in heaven. Ought to stop giving her shit for that.

"You want some ants on a log?" Stella asks me.

"Don't you need peanut butter for that?"

"We can do it with hummus!" she announces, taking a stalk of celery and scooping some hummus onto it. "Hmm. No raisins. Grapes!"

I grimace. "Grapes, hummus, and celery. Sounds...delightful."

Gillian giggles. "I'll be your taste tester if you're nervous."

"My hero," I reply.

She smiles, holding her chin in the air.

Stella finishes her concoction and holds it up for Gillian to take a bite. "It's good! I promise."

"You haven't even tasted it," Gillian says back.

The little girl giggles. Seeing them face to face is like seeing both sides of a mirror. They're alike in all ways except for their eyes. Stella guides the celery up to Gillian's mouth. She's braver than I am as she munches on the Frankenstein treat. "Mm," Gillian says with a nod. "Not bad, actually."

"Are you pretending?" I ask.

"No, not at all. You should try it."

I notice there's a splotch of hummus on the corner of Gillian's mouth. "You've got a..." I gesture to my mouth.

She blushes. "Oh." She touches the other side of her mouth. "Hummus?"

"No, here, let me–" I reach out and swipe the hummus away from her lips, my fingers naturally resting against her jaw.

I freeze when our eyes meet. Dear god, it would be so easy to kiss her right now.

And Gillian's not drawing away from me. She feels it too. I'm almost sure of it. It would be wrong to kiss her here, right in front of her daughter and in front of all her friends when we've made it very clear to one another that this is just a friendship.

However, now, more than ever, it's clear to me that I can't handle just a friendship with Gillian. I want more. Need more.

I need all of her.

"Napkin!" Stella shouts out, interrupting our moment.

I jerk away from Gillian and take the napkin from Stella. "Thank you, Stella."

"Okay, your turn!" She holds the bitten celery stalk up toward me.

I sneer at the snack. "I'm not biting the part your mom just bit. What if I get cooties?"

"What are cooties?"

"They're–"

"Axel," Gillian whispers. "Cooties aren't a thing anymore."

I frown. "What?!"

"It's like...not politically correct."

I nod slowly. "Oh, I see. Never mind."

Stella huffs, "What are cooties?! I want to know."

"No such thing," I shrug and then take a bite of the celery even though Gillian took a bite already. "Mm! Delicious. You were right!" I'm not tasting a thing, though. My brain is too fired up on thoughts of Gillian and how ill-prepared I am for a life with a child, because I know that by pursuing Gillian, Stella is part of the package. And that doesn't scare me.

What scares me is that I'd be bad at taking care of her.

Gillian laughs, "See, I told you!"

"Eat the rest!" Stella announces and shoves it toward my mouth.

The rest of the meal, I can't shake the feeling I had about Gillian. It feels like my body is buzzing. That something has been initiated between us.

I remember this feeling.

I had it seven years ago. Something too scary to speak of exists between us, but I need to follow through. I need to know if on the other side of it is a reality where I can have Gillian. Not just behind closed doors. But for the whole world to know.

Here on the blanket with Stella is a very good start.

19

GILLIAN

WE ARE SOME OF THE LAST PEOPLE TO LEAVE THE LOT as golden hour sets in upon us. The time has just flown. I can barely believe it. Between Stella running around enjoying games with friends to talking with other parents, I feel like I blinked and almost missed everything.

Not to mention having Axel at my side is...nice.

Not just nice.

I love it.

Despite his enemy status to most of the parents at Seton, he managed to talk them down from skewering him with a pitchfork by telling them about his ideas for a community park. I can barely believe it myself. In fact, I'm a little suspicious he's just saying things so that he isn't public enemy number one.

However, as much as I don't want to admit it, I know Axel. At least pieces of him. I know when he's being earnest. And the way that he's talking about the park and explaining what he thinks he might be able to accomplish with it just screams earnest Axel Hitchins.

Still, though, he's betrayed me before. He's more than capable of doing it again.

After our picnic is cleaned up, Stella leads us back to Axel's car, waltzing from side to side, a butterfly painted on each of her cheeks.

"How does she have so much energy?" Axel asks.

"She's six," I reply.

He grins at me.

It makes my heart plummet into my stomach.

We drive back in relative quiet, except for the radio, which Axel tunes to a top forty station. Stella sings along to all the songs, even though most of the lyrics are wrong (and given how raunchy things can be on the radio, I'm grateful).

When we arrive at the bakery, the closed sign is already flipped, and I can see Lola inside mopping.

"Well, Stella, what do you say?" I ask.

"Oh, thank you!" Stella cries out, poking her head between the front seats. "Thank you for coming."

Axel grins. "You're welcome."

"Did you have fun?" she asks.

"Oh, loads."

Stella looks at me, her nose in the air. "See, Mommy? I knew he'd have a good time."

I smile. "Guess you were right."

"I usually am," she remarks and then jumps out of the car, rushing inside the bakery to greet Lola.

This leaves us in a tremendous vacuum of silence I wish I could escape.

And yet...at the same time, I never want to leave.

Being alone with Axel feels good for the first time in a long time.

"Thanks for letting me tag along, Gillian."

I half-laugh, "Don't thank me. You're the one who walked right into what could have been your demise. It was impressive."

Axel shakes his head and looks off through the dashboard with a soft smile.

"Did you mean what you were saying about the park?" I ask carefully.

He bites on his lower lip and I prepare to be disappointed. Of course he didn't mean it. He was just trying to make everybody feel better since he had tagged along to an event he was never supposed to be at in a million years. Surely, he would have no way of changing everything just to make a measly little park instead of –

"It'll take some work, but it's the right thing to do," he replies and then casts a look my way.

Don't look at me. I might just have to kiss you.

"I mean, you know my dad, it might take a while but–"

"As long as you meant it. Even if it doesn't pan out, I just needed to know you meant it."

Our eyes lock. I want to kiss him so bad. But Lola is *literally* just inside. It was one thing to have an affair when she was overseas. Now, though, it would be cruel to betray her when she's merely twenty feet away.

"I meant it, Gill," he says in a voice so tender I know it's only meant for my ears.

Fuck. Get out of here. "Well, thanks again. For the ride," I mutter and then push open my door.

"Any time," he calls after me.

I close the door and scurry inside before he can say anything else. I don't dare look back at him either. Just seeing him staring at me out his window would have me running right back to him. "Hey! How was the afternoon here?" I cry out as I walk into the bakery.

"Good! Just finished with the mopping and bagging up the extras. We'll drop them off at the shelter on our way to dinner," Lola explains as she throws a couple croissants into a brown paper bag.

I totally forgot that Lola and Stella are supposed to have dinner tonight together. Lola is Stella's godmother, and she takes the role *extremely* seriously. They have dates every month where Stella is allowed to say whatever she wants about whomever she wants because "children need to have an outlet" (that's Lola's excuse). What's worse is their dates are in a bubble of silence, meaning I never hear anything about it. I fear that Stella is ranting and raving about my parenting skills while Lola pours her another glass of wine and says, "Tell me more."

Okay, I don't actually fear the wine. But I do wonder what Lola knows about my daughter's feelings that I don't.

Stella sits on the counter, her legs kicking back and forth over the edge. "Where are we going tonight?"

"Hmmm...pizza or burgers?"

"Burgers! Please burgers!" Stella cries out.

"Is that alright with you, Mom?" Lola asks.

"More than. You two go to town," I say. I do my best as a vegan to deal with the trials of raising my child eating animal products. Beef is where I draw the line. Especially burger meat. You're telling me ground up, red animal chunks are appealing to people? *Please.* Makes me gag just looking at it. "You can even have a milkshake."

Lola and Stella exchange a look of excitement. "Seriously? That's a lot of sugar," Lola says. Stella pokes Lola on the arm. *Don't say that or she won't let me have one!*

I laugh, "It's Saturday. It's fine." Plus, we've already arranged for Dana to look after Stella at our dad's house afterward so I can get started on getting our financials for taxes this upcoming quarter. When you run a small business, every time you turn around it's tax time again. Drives me crazy.

"You heard the woman! Burgers and milkshakes for all!" Lola announces and lifts Stella off the counter and takes her by the hand. "You all good here, Gillian?"

"Right as rain. You two have fun."

Stella comes up to me and hugs me. "Bye, Mommy. See you later."

I wrap my arms around her; I can smell the whole day in her hair. Grass and sweat and dirt. Just a kid being a kid, not knowing how complicated everything else is. I hope I can protect her for as long as possible. "See you tonight. Be good."

Lola and Stella walk hand in hand to Lola's car. I wave at them through the window and then lock the bakery door behind me. I'm in for a long night of number crunching, so I pour myself a cup of coffee and get to work.

I hole up in the office and go through more excel sheets than I ever thought I'd have to in my adult life. Number crunching isn't a fun job, but between Lola and me, I make less errors which means less time we have to pay a tax specialist. Helps out in the long run.

After about an hour, I'm sitting in silence staring in frustration as the numbers aren't adding up. I hear a soft knock. I look out through the office door which gives me a clear view of the front door. No one is there. They must be at the back door.

And hell if I'm going to open the back door of the bakery when I'm here alone.

However, whoever is out there is persistent. They knock again.

I swallow. What the hell could anyone want with a bakery after hours unless they wanted to rob the place or hurt someone?

I reach into the bottom drawer of the desk and pull out a canister of pepper spray. If I'm going to answer the door, I'm going to be prepared.

I creep into the hallway and stare at the back door. For a cute bakery, the back door is ugly. Dark gray with a crash bar spanning the width of it. We've never gotten around to painting it in the light blue and green color scheme of the rest of the place. After all, we're the only people who see it. However, right now, I'm wishing it was a friendly color rather than dark and ominous.

As I walk toward the door, there's another knock and I practically leap out of my skin. "Who's there?"

There's a muffled response.

Dammit. I'm going to have to open the damn door.

I creep up to the door, press on the latch, and open it just an inch. "I have pepper spray and a gun, so–"

"Whoa, whoa, whoa!" I hear Axel's voice on the other side. "Gillian, it's me!"

I open the door fully. "What are you doing here?!" I cry out. "You scared me half to death."

"Sorry, I'm just–" He shoves his hands in his pockets. "The front was locked and I..." He trails off and frowns. "You have a gun?"

I stand up straighter. "No. Just the pepper spray," I say, holding up the pink plastic cannister.

We stare at each other. He hasn't given me a reason for being here and I'm not sure I'm going to get one. At least not in words.

"Lola's gone?"

"Yes."

"And Stella..."

"They're at dinner. What's going on? Is something wrong?"

Axel doesn't reply. But there's a look in his eye...I've seen it so many times before. Desperate and needy. Trying to figure out how to ask for what he wants.

He's caught me on a good day. Because I'm powerless to withhold anything from him. "Well, do you want to come inside? You're letting in a–"

I don't even have a chance to finish my sentence before Axel's lips are on mine. I immediately melt, powerless to do anything but let his lips do their magic. His arms slide around me, clutching me to his chest. I throw down the can of pepper spray and grab onto his collar. Need meets need.

"Gillian, I–"

"You don't have to explain," I say, panting hungrily. "Come inside."

Axel ignores the double entendre and pushes me through the door and against the wall. The tension is so high that we are both struggling to know what to do with ourselves. As soon as I grab one part of him, my brain remembers another. I rake my hands through his hair, slide my hands over his shoulder blades, press my hips into his.

God, I feel him. So hard and wanting for me.

"I have to have you," he murmurs and then presses a kiss to my neck. "I'll die without you."

I would laugh if I could. It's an absurd statement. Except, I feel it just as deeply.

Axel's hands slide under my flannel shirt. As soon as his fingers glance against my bare skin, I'm a puddle on the floor. I can feel the temperature rising between my thighs, my muscles contracting, desperate to invite him inside.

It hasn't even been five minutes.

I push Axel against the opposite wall. He gasps in surprise. But this is not about control. This is about need. I pull his shirt up over his head, not paying any heed to the couple of buttons that leap off. As soon as he throws it to the ground, our lips are locked again.

Axel pushes his hands into the waistband of my shorts and forces me backward toward the door of the office. "Where can I have you?" he whispers.

"Wherever you want."

He laughs against my lips. "Déjà vu."

I laugh too. For once, the memory of our dalliance isn't tinged with ache and disappointment. It's a reminder of the amazing days and nights we spent together, exploring each other, taking care of each other in ways we never had.

We can have that again.

I land against the door just as he jerks my shorts downward. His hands slip up from my waist to my chest, caressing my breasts as he hungrily kisses me. Each kiss is sending me higher and higher, like a drug that just won't quit. I don't feel like I'm on this planet anymore. Nothing else exists except Axel's lips, hands, and...

"C'mere," he huffs, pulling me into the office. He positions me with my hips against the desk and his cock wanting at my backside. I place my hands on the desk, awaiting his entrance. Instead, though, Axel slides his hand around my jaw and guides my face toward his. "Just look at me."

I find my eyes locked once again in his enigmatic green orbs. They are hypnotic. Never seen anything like them. Until Stella, of course. I swallow.

"Look at me the whole time, Gillian," he whispers.

I feel his cock sliding in and out from between my thighs, enjoying my warmth and wetness. His eyes, though, do not leave mine, even as it becomes harder and harder to maintain control.

I do the same, not daring to look away. "Inside," I whisper, pressing my mouth into his hand. "I need you inside."

I push my hips back against his, the head of his cock nudging my entrance. Axel's brow bends and he bites his lower lip. I can already tell how good it feels for him. He slides in just a bit deeper and then swears.

"It's okay," I whisper, leaning back against him. Now his lips are only a kiss away from mine.

"You just feel so good, I'm afraid I'll lose it too fast and I'll–"

"Axel, honey, I don't care," I cut him off. Unlike the last time we fucked, this isn't about getting what's mine. This isn't about the anger that's been brewing between us all these years.

It's about our bodies being together. Whatever that looks like is enough for me.

"*I* care, Gillian. I want to make you feel good, I've always..." he trails off. He knows he can't finish that sentence and it be true. He has done too many things to hurt me for him to always have wanted to make me feel good.

"It's alright–"

"It's not," he hisses in response. One of his hands slides down to my pelvis and skims my clitoris. "All I want is to make you feel good. That's all that matters to me."

Without realizing it, we've begun to rock together. Simultaneously, Axel starts to work on my clitoris with a tender touch. There are so many things I want to say to him, but none that would make sense to say right now as we are cornered in the throes of pleasure.

Axel's other hand digs into my stomach, fingers curling

with possession. He doesn't have to say that I'm his to make it true.

It may only be for this moment. But I have to hope it will be for much longer.

His pace quickens and he has to drop his head to my shoulder. "Oh fuck."

"You feel so good," I whisper. My body knows him so well. And his cock manages to stretch me out and make a home inside me in record time. "You feel so amazing."

Axel wraps his arms up the front of my chest, his hands clenched in fists right at my sternum. I lean forward and grab the edge of the desk. He thrusts into me, sending longing breaths from me each time.

"Yes, that's it," I whisper. "Deeper."

He pushes himself all the way to the hilt, impossibly deep inside me, and I let out a primal screech, overwhelmed at the delicious feeling of his cock all the way inside me. Axel latches a hand to my thigh for leverage and fucks me faster. His lips are pressed together right by my ear; I hear his tremulous humming as he tries to stay steady for me.

I press my forehead to the side of his head, gasping for air. "Axel..."

"Say my name."

"Axel..."

"It sounds so good in your mouth."

"Axel, Axel, Axel," I repeat, each mention of his name paired with a kiss.

Suddenly, he wraps his hand around the back of my head, snapping our eyes back together. His are wild, like an animal. He grunts loudly, driving his hips faster and faster.

The warmth is growing inside me at a rapid pace. My jaw falls open as a moan forms at the base of my throat.

"Yes, baby. Yes. Let me make you feel good."

Rivers of pleasure flow through my body, blood rushing at a record pace, swelling right in the pit of my belly. "Axell-ll..." I moan warningly.

"Come for me, baby. Let it all out."

He grabs onto the shelf above the desk and uses it to help him drive his hips harder. I'm a slave to his speed and his rhythm; only a moment later, a shockwave violently snaps inside me. The tension releases and the red heat of my orgasm blisters through me. I scream, clutching at the desk to steady me. My legs are jelly, shaking with euphoria.

"Good girl, good girl, that's it, that's–" Axel is cut off by a sharp inhale and then lets out a nonsensical cry, his head dropping to my shoulder. I feel him release deep inside me, not for a second flinching from this communion. "Oh my god," he whispers and wraps his hands around my belly. I can feel his heaving breaths traveling down my back. "You feel so good, Gillian, you make me feel so..." He sighs heavily. "Oh my god."

I smile to myself, pulses of pleasure still echoing through my body. I reach over my shoulder and run my hand through his dark hair. It's soft but damp with sweat. "You worked so hard," I murmur and kiss his brow.

Axel chuckles and then kisses my back. "Of course I did." His hands caress my hips, and he repeats gently, "Of course I did, Gillian."

I let the afterglow wash over us. So unlike the last time we fucked when I kicked him out immediately. No, this time I want to bask in it.

Axel embraces me from behind and takes a deep whiff of my hair. Then, he says something that makes my heart stop. "Anything for you, Gillian."

Anything?

It's time to find out if Axel Hitchins is true to his word.

Because if he says anything, I *want* anything.

Actually, I want his everything.

20

———

AXEL

I had to come back for her.

I couldn't leave Gillian after that. Pretend that I've just been fine inside, life as normal.

Nothing has been normal between us. For years, really. And today, it boiled over inside me.

I had intended to come to explain myself and where I stood. How I feel about her. What I want. But the second I saw her standing there with her pepper spray, ready to kick a guy in the nuts if she had to, I just had to have her. I couldn't hold myself back.

Now, here she is, in my arms, her breath steadying. I've just told her I'll give her everything and I mean it from the bottom of my soul.

"You want some water?" she asks in a raspy voice.

I don't want her to leave me.

"I'm so thirsty."

But I can't make her stay. "S-sure."

We unlock from one another; my body recoils against the cold air, the feeling of not being inside her.

"Be right back," she says shyly with a small smile before disappearing through the office door.

I'm suddenly hit with a memory of our time together, seven years ago. The first time. At my house. I was staying there alone for the week while my dad was on a business trip. Obviously, Lola was out of the country. And Jeremiah and Dad had just had their blowup a few months before. Just me. Gillian would come by to keep me company. One thing led to another and...then we were in my bed.

That first time, once we were finished, she slipped out of bed, offered to get me water. I was such a selfish guy I let her. At *my* house. Not that she didn't know every nook and cranny already from having spent nearly half her childhood at our house to hang out with Lola.

"Gillian, wait," I say, going after her.

I'm a little too late. She's already grabbing water from the tap in the bakery proper. Outside, the sun is merely an ember on the horizon. "Hm? What is it?" she asks.

I just stare at her for a minute. I'm ready to be a grown man about this. It's taken me long enough.

Gillian narrows her eyes. "You okay?"

I swallow.

"Here, have some water."

"No," I say too forcefully. "I mean..."

"Axel, what's wrong?"

"I fucked up," I finally say. "I've *been* fucking up for a long time now."

Gillian gives me a cocked smile and comes over to me, putting the water glass on the counter beside me for me to take. "Is this your new postcoital pillow talk? Because it's *definitely* working..." she jokes.

I'd laugh if my heart wasn't spiraling into ribbons.

"Gillian, listen. What I did...all those years ago. It wasn't right."

Her smile falls and she looks away. "Oh."

I wish she'd say more.

"Water under the bridge," she says and starts to retreat back into the office.

"No, come on." I grab her by the wrist before she can walk away. "I'm not completely heartless, Gillian. I know I hurt you."

Her eyes widen. "You *know* you hurt me?"

It's clear I don't know the extent to which I have, based on her tone of voice.

Gillian jerks her hand away from me. "You don't even know the half of it, Axel."

"I know I don't. I'm sorry."

She flinches. "That's a lot of good, seven years later."

"Hey..." I say softly. "I have no excuses. I have nothing to offer you except that I'm here to listen and own up to my actions now."

Gillian stares at me, her brown eyes flickering. Are those tears in her eyes? I can't tell in the shadowy light. "Axel, just because we weren't supposed to have feelings for each other didn't mean that I could just stop them from happening, alright?"

My heart gallops in my chest. That was our deal. That first time was so good we wanted to keep having fun. Sex, no string attached. We both needed it. I needed a release from the stress my dad was putting on me. And Gillian needed a way to get over her ex-boyfriend, Martin Holtz. We were using each other. At least that's how it started. Foolish to think that after so many years of knowing each other the feelings wouldn't inevitably follow.

"But I took that on the chin. I was willing to swallow it

and just...move on." Her cheeks grow tight. "But for you to do what you did—"

"I'm so sorry."

"To just...act like I didn't even exist—"

"It was wrong."

"You wouldn't even look at me," she finishes. And that's when the tears spill down her face. "God, this is so stupid." She looks away, covering her eyes.

I've never felt good about my decision. The days just ticked down so quickly and my feelings were so out of control I thought the only way to deal with it was... pretending like nothing had happened. I was so young back then. At least...I feel like I was younger. It's not an excuse. Especially if she's been carrying the hurt with her all these years.

The truth is, I hurt both of us. That was when I decided to throw myself at the family business, at our legacy. Wasn't going to let a woman get in my way, especially not a woman I knew might take my whole heart and soul with her if I wasn't careful. And a woman I was never supposed to have to begin with.

"It was wrong of me to do that," I say with a stiff upper lip. "I should have told you how I really felt."

Gillian wipes the tears off her face. "I might be crying, but I promise I'm over it, okay? We don't have to rehash this; I know you didn't come here for—"

"Gillian, listen to me," I say and come toward her, taking her hand in mine. I feel her pull away at first, but then she relaxes into my touch. "This is exactly what I came here for."

She furrows her brow with curiosity.

"I was...a coward back then. Not because I didn't want

to hurt you or let you down easy, but because I was falling in love with you."

Her eyes widen.

"How was I supposed to say anything when we'd agreed it would be nothing? And then Lola came home and–" *Don't chicken out. Man up and own up to your mistakes.* "I was too scared to tell you the truth because...because I was too scared to tell you."

Gillian's lips creep upward even though tears are still tumbling down her face.

"I thought I was choosing my family by pushing you away. Because I couldn't imagine how we would make it work. Between Lola and the pressure my dad was putting on me to take over for Jeremiah, it was–"

"You were so stressed," she says.

A knife to the heart. She remembers, no doubt, staying up late with me as I rambled about my fears of the future. How the music played in the background and our limbs wove together. Gillian held me. And listened. Kissed my forehead.

And what did I do? I acted like she didn't exist.

"I didn't deserve you then. I don't deserve you now," I say carefully, then wrap my other hand around hers. "But I'm not going to be a coward anymore." I look her dead in the eye. "I want to be with you, Gillian."

She starts to smile, but something isn't letting her. "Axel, I'm not the same girl."

"I know you're not."

"I'm a mom now."

I smile, thinking of Stella. As if I haven't considered her as part of the whole thing. "I know that, Gillian."

"So, it'd be crazy to think that we could have anything like we had back then because–"

"I'm not asking for what we had back then. I was a selfish and immature brat who didn't know how to talk about his emotions, so I ended up hurting the only girl I ever–" I choke back the word "loved". Too soon. Not sure if I'm ready for that word to slip out of my mouth. "...ever cared about."

Gillian doesn't say anything, but she doesn't have to. Her expression says everything. Sweet smile, eyes only for me.

"I've watched you grow up. It's my fault it was from afar. But I want to be a part of your life from now on, the way I've *always* wanted to be."

Though her smile grows, more tears stream down her cheeks.

"Is that crazy?"

Gillian grabs my face and kisses me. Her lips are planted to mine, ready to take root. I slide my hands around her waist. That's where she's always been meant to be, in my arms like this. After a long kiss, she pulls away. "Yes, it's crazy."

I laugh. "Oh, damn."

She kisses me again and leans her forehead against mine. "And I feel the same way."

Even though she's just kissed me, I can barely believe she's said it. That she's willing to go there with me after everything I've done to her. Gillian Solace is an amazing woman, willing to give up the tension of seven years, anger, frustration, betrayal, and give me a chance. "Really?"

Gillian nods. "Yes, really."

I run my fingers through her dirty blonde hair. I can hardly believe I'm standing with her here in the dark having just poured my soul out to her. After all these years, it feels like the greatest weight has been lifted off my back.

From her place in my arms, Gillian takes the glass of water and sips. "I really need this now."

"Me too."

She places it against my lips and tips it back. I drink from it, relishing her giggle. A little water dribbles out on my chin. "Careful," I gurgle.

Gillian wipes off my chin with her finger, so tenderly I feel faint. "Don't change your mind on me now, okay?"

"No way. Now that you're right here...never letting you go, Gill."

She kisses my cheek and then burrows her head in my neck. We stand like this for a long time. The reality is setting in that we are...I guess we're together now. It's the most amazing feeling I've ever had. My only regret is I waited this long to let it happen.

"We'll have to tell Stella eventually," she says. "And what she thinks and wants is most important to me, so—"

"Something tells me I'm not going to have to worry about Stella liking having me around," I say. "It's my *sister* I'm worried about."

Gillian groans into my neck. "Why are you bringing Lola up at a time like this?"

"Because she's part of the reason it's taken us this long to do this in the first place?"

Gillian smiles sneakily. "Do what?"

"You know."

"Say it."

I roll my eyes, but I can't stop smiling. "Get together..."

Then she squeals. "Yes! Oh, that sounds so good. I love when you say it." She peppers my face with kisses. "Axel and Gillian sitting in a tree..."

"Okay, how old are you?"

"Nearly thirty. But you, old man —"

"Don't start with the over thirty business, missy."

We both laugh, holding each other closely. I cup Gillian's face in my hand and stroke the sticky tracks of tears on her face. Nearly faded, but a reminder of the sadness past. "We'll tell Lola together, huh?"

"And what if she's mad?" Gillian asks, eyes downcast. "She's going to be so upset with me."

"She'll be upset with *us*," I say. "Together."

She looks back at me, corner of her lip turned upward.

"Besides, we're adults. She has to understand we're living our lives." I take a deep breath. "And Gillian, I am willing to fight for you. I am willing to go to hell and back for you." I pull her hand to my mouth and kiss her knuckles. "I promise."

Gillian considers me a moment. "I promise too," she says and then kisses my knuckles in return.

Nothing has ever made me feel more like a man than a kiss to the knuckles by the woman I can picture myself with for a long, long time.

21

GILLIAN

I can't stop smiling. My cheeks hurt.

Axel is mine. At least for now.

And I wasn't crazy. All those years ago, those feelings I was having for him, he was having too. It breaks my heart that we spent seven years nursing this anguish when we could have been together.

Stella could have had a father.

But that's a matter that's still too complicated for me to even broach. One thing at a time.

Axel and I spend the next hour eating a quick cookie dough I whip up from scratch. "It tastes like the real thing," he marvels.

"It *is* the real thing," I reply.

He rolls his eyes. "I'm going to be eating a lot more vegan food, aren't I?"

"As long as you keep an open mind," I retort, swiping a bit of cookie dough onto his nose.

He gasps and lunges for me. It turns into an all-out chase around the bakery until I breathlessly give up, laughing as he pulls me into his arms and kisses me, the cookie dough now on my nose too. "If you think you can get away from me, Gillian, you are sorely mistaken. Because from now on..." he murmurs, "You are mine."

I sigh in ecstasy. *Is this real life? I must be dreaming.*

Things are more complicated now. There's a child to deal with (one he doesn't yet know is his) and there is the matter of Lola...

However, we are touching each other freely. Even seven years ago we weren't able to do that. Our interactions were always tinged with illicitness. Now...it's real. Axel has made it known he's willing to fight for me. And I'm willing to fight for him too.

Time ticks down quicker than either of us would like and soon enough it's nearly ten o'clock. "Told Dana I'd be by to get Stella by nine..." I whisper to Axel. We're sitting on the floor of the office, backs against the wall, our hands intertwined.

"Tell her you're busy," he replies and kisses my jaw.

"If only it were that easy." I think for a moment. "It's different now. I told you it would be different."

Axel chuckles, "Oh, Gillian. Why do you say that like you're expecting me to run away from you?"

Because I am. Because you did. I hold those thoughts back. They'll do no good now that we're here.

I've managed all these years to remain hopeful that someone would come along. The right man. The one who wouldn't care that I already had a daughter and would fit into my life easily enough that it would just make sense. Against all odds, I've carried this hope. Heartbroken too many times to count, even before Axel, starting with my mother, sometimes I wonder if I have any business at all remaining hopeful.

But I'm glad I did.

Without that hope I wouldn't have gotten here with Axel.

I rest my head on his shoulder and feel him kiss the top of my head.

"I know you have to go. It's okay."

I grab tightly to his arm and sigh. "I wish I didn't have to."

"I'll see you soon. Tomorrow, if you'll let me."

I smile and nod, but then remember, "Stella has a dentist appointment tomorrow. And then I'm helping Harley with planning the reception. Monday."

"Monday."

"Or wait, on Monday–"

Axel touches my chin. "As soon as I can see you, I want to see you. How about that?"

From somewhere in the room, I hear the buzzing of the phone. I lift my head. "Yours or mine?"

Axel reaches into his pocket and holds up his phone. Screen is black. Mine.

"It's probably Dana calling, wondering where I am," I grumble and get to my feet. I find my phone by the light beaming from the screen, still strewn on the desk where I left it before Axel so wonderfully intruded. But it's not Dana's name on the screen. "It's Kira."

"Let it go to voicemail."

"You know I can't do that."

He grins. "Worth a shot."

I smile at him though my heart is pumping. Kira is not the calling late in the evening type. If she needs to communicate over something other than a text, she'll plan a phone call, even if it's fifteen minutes in the future. The only other reason she would call me out of the blue is if I've butt-dialed her by accident, as I am wont to do. I answer tentatively. "Hello?"

"Gillian!" Kira shouts. There's the thrum of loud music and people shouting in the background "I need to talk to you!"

"Where are you? It's so loud, I can barely hear you!" I reply.

"Wait a second, I'm trying to get outside—excuse me!" she shouts through what I imagine to be a throng of people. Slowly but surely, the background noise lessons until it's barely anything at all. "Sorry, I'm at this thing for work."

"Where is it? Coachella?" I say humorously.

Kira doesn't laugh. "I don't know, some club in the valley. It's a birthday party for one of the execs and I had to go and—" She stops and grunts. "That's not the point."

This isn't like Kira. Talking too fast and stumbling over her words. That only happens when something has happened. Something big. I glance back at Axel who is doing something on his phone in an attempt not to listen. I'll make it easy for him and go out into the bakery. "Kira, what's wrong?"

"Are you sitting down?"

"No."

"Well, you should sit down."

"Are you drunk?"

Kira sighs. "A couple of drinks."

"Do you need me to come pick you up?"

"Gillian, no! *I'm* fine! This is about *you!*"

I pause and lean against the counter. What the hell would have to do with me at her work event at a club in the valley? "You're scaring me."

"I want to start off by apologizing."

"Oh my god, Kira, what's going *on*?!"

"I ran into Martin."

My heart drops. "What?"

"He was at the club. I don't know who with or–that doesn't matter."

Martin Holtz. A name I hear so rarely. He was the reason Axel and I fell together in the first place. At least he was my reason. He'd broken my heart into smithereens right before the summer started. Hot girl summer went out the window. I was distraught. Thought I'd marry the man.

He has served as Stella's father in my narrative. The perfect scapegoat. In the distress of finding out I was pregnant, I created a fake narrative. That we'd had one last time together that summer and it had to be him.

That was a lie. I haven't seen Martin since the day he broke up with me.

"Anyway, I'm drinking, right. So, I see him and I go up to him and ask if he remembers me."

I cover my face in horror. "Kira, you didn't."

"And he didn't. Of course he didn't. Because he's a piece of shit. So, I told him who I was."

"Oh *no*."

"And...this is the part that you need to be sitting down for."

The anticipation is literally killing me.

"I told him that he could go to hell for what he did and he..."

No...

"He had no idea what I was talking about." Kira gulps in some air. "So, I was like, 'Leaving my sister to have your baby all by herself?!'"

This is it. This is my downfall.

"He was shocked. He didn't know."

I lied to everyone. I told them I'd tried to talk to him and he said he wanted nothing to do with me. With the baby. My dad wanted to chase him down and make him step up. I told him not to. I'd do it without him.

Because...he didn't deserve to be implicated any further in my lie, even if he'd broken my heart.

"Didn't you tell him, Gillian? You said you told him."

I shake my head even though she can't see me and finally ask in a strangled voice, "What did he say?"

Now, Axel peeks his head out from the back, a look of concern on his face. *Shit.*

"He stormed off. He didn't say anything."

Axel takes a step forward and mouths, "Is everything okay?"

Why does the timing of my life have to be so piss poor? Or so serendipitous it sometimes feels like I'm a character in someone's computer game and they're just putting me in absolutely insane situations? Here I am, on the phone, talking about the man I pretended to be the father of my child while the actual father of my child is standing here not *knowing* he's the father of my child.

This mess is all my fault.

"I'm so sorry, Gillian," Kira says.

"It's okay, it's my fault," I murmur, turning away from Axel.

"No, it's not. You were put in an impossible situation. I don't blame you for never telling him."

I can feel a migraine coming on. I shut my eyes tight. "Thanks for telling me."

Axel touches my back. My brain is telling me to push him away, but my heart wants nothing more than to be as close to him as possible.

"Listen, I have to go," I say to Kira. "I have to pick up

Stella from Dad's and–anyway, have fun. Don't worry about this, alright?"

"Gillian–"

"*Have fun*," I reiterate, forcing a smile. "I mean it."

"...okay."

We say our goodbyes and we hang up. Axel is still behind me, his hand softly sliding up and down my back.

"What's wrong, Gill?"

I flip around abruptly with a smile on my face and roll my eyes. "Kira's boss wanted to move his party here so that he could have some late-night snacks or something. I don't know. I had to tell her we were closed and he's going to flip out at her and, well, I feel terrible so–"

From the look on Axel's face, I can tell he doesn't believe me.

"I need to go get Stella," I say with finality.

Though I can see the questions swirling in his eyes, he nods. "Of course. Would you call me when you get home?"

"I will."

"And if she's up, tell her I say hi. Or good night."

My heart swells and I feel like I could burst into tears all over again. "Sounds good. She'll like that."

Axel smiles. The corners of his eyes are tired. "Good." He leans in and kisses me softly. "Good night, Gillian."

I wish I could throw my arms around him and never let him go. But I can't. There's a humongous secret sitting between us. And until I tell him, I can't have him the way I need him.

Axel leaves out the back and I'm left alone with all my thoughts.

I never thought I'd be ready for the truth.

And I'm not ready now.

However, I think it's time. I have to throw myself off the cliff and take the risk.

I need to tell Axel the truth about Stella.

22

———

AXEL

I have a spring in my step walking into the Hitchins corporate office. I've never felt this good on a Monday morning. Never felt like I could conquer the world like I can now.

Now that I have Gillian, I feel like I can do anything.

Our communication has been sparse over the past two days, but I'm not worrying about it. She's a mother. She's busy. And I've got my own hide to worry about today. Dad and I have a meeting with our shareholders and I'm about to drop a bombshell on them all.

My briefcase holds the drafts for a park on the Seton lot. I got into contact with a park architect just yesterday and paid them an absurd amount to get me a draft by this morning. The guy came through and it's better than I could have even imagined. I sent a picture to Gillian before I left and she gushed about over text with heart eyes and applauding hands.

I nearly fainted.

Who is this man and what did he do with the old Axel Hitchins?

That guy, that hopeless and cynical one, I hope is long gone. I've got hopes and dreams and they begin and end with Gillian.

The in between is what I have to worry about.

"Perfect timing," my dad mutters as I slink into the elevator just before it closes.

"Morning," I say, immediately feeling my blood run cold. It does feel a bit like a betrayal that I'm going to go in here with new plans before even running them by my dad. However, I'm giving him what he's wanted: I'm going to take charge. "Nice weekend?"

"Fine. Hip is acting up again."

I smile at my father. He's started shrinking. When I was a child, he felt so big. Now, he's seventy years old and hunching over. "You should get that replacement."

"Who has the time?"

He does. But it's not time that's the problem. He's scared. "You can take a couple months off and recover. Or, better yet, retire."

Dad shoots daggers at me. "You trying to get rid of me?"

The elevator dings and the doors slide open at the executive floor. I shake my head. "Not at all. Just a thought."

I stride out ahead of him, not bothering to look back.

If Dad wants me to take charge, then it's going to happen when he least expects it.

Make way, because Axel Hitchins is ready for a fight.

"This proposal is not what you have been expecting. We at Hitchins are looking to go bigger and better than ever before," I announce as I ready my slideshow.

The shareholders all look quite excited, which for

mostly men over fifty with hair coming out of their ears, is hard to discern to the untrained eye. But I can tell, having been around people like this my whole life. It's the slight upturn of their lips and the lift of their chin that tells me I've got them right where I want them.

Dad is also watching me with hawkish attention.

Come on, Axel. Pull the rug out from under them.

"Our project has not been without controversy and community consternation. I had the distinct privilege of being invited to participate in a community event this past Saturday. It was an opportunity for me to see past the protesting and actually understand where the Seton Elementary community was coming from."

I lift the clicker up toward the projector. "Our new proposal might feel uncomfortable at first. But even good things feel wrong when we aren't used to them. All I ask is you give me the opportunity to subvert your expectations."

Out of the corner of my eye, I see my dad's brow flinch. *It's only going to get worse from here, Daddio.*

"This –" I press the clicker and the slide changes to an image of a park with kids running around and parents sitting chatting. "Is the Seton Play Lot."

The room of shareholders stares at me dumbfounded. I can't read their expressions beyond their confusion. Good confused, bad confused? I'm not sure.

I expected this, though. This is a complete one-eighty from everything we've been pitching them about the Seton lot condos. It's understandable they'll need some time to adjust.

"A *park?*" my dad growls.

"You could call it that."

He gapes at me and then turns around to look at the shareholders. "Gentlemen, I assure you he's joking."

"And *I* can assure you, I'm not." I click to the next slide that has the plans I commissioned yesterday. "As you can see here, the Seton Play Lot gives Hitchins the opportunity to be on the forefront of the community care movement. In our digital age, we are lacking third and even second spaces. We have our homes, a first space. Some of us have our workplaces. A second. But what are our third spaces? Libraries and parks remain two of the only free and accessible places for people to commune together."

"Accessibility is not—" my dad starts to huff.

"By investing in projects like this, Hitchins is given an opportunity to continue in the residential sector while taking a fresh stance on the role of corporations in our communities. This balance will save us future protests and scandals like we've had with this one. And it will also allow us to be a part of the communities that we claim to want to create," I explain.

"*Axel*," Dad snaps. "That is enough."

I look at him with a blank expression. This is the boardroom. Not our house. And he should have the respect and grace to treat it as such. "I have the floor, Father."

A flash of fear enters his eyes. "This is not what we discussed."

"I know. You've wanted me to be more proactive and care more about the business. That's what I'm doing." I look back at the investors with a smile. "I'm much more interested in hearing what you gentlemen think at this point."

They all exchange fearful looks. Who is going to speak first? Who is going to take the risk?

"I like it," one of them finally says. He's our most established investor, been with us the longest. In fact, he's known me since I was just a little kid. "I think it's a big swing. Could be a homerun."

I nod. "Thank you, sir."

"My question, though–" someone else pipes up, "is once the facility is built, who takes care of the upkeep and how does it make money?"

I smile. "Well, gentlemen, this is where you all come in. We are in an age where the wealthy are in a constant moral quandary. I believe with limited term investments; the Seton Play Lot can serve as a way for investors to get involved in an immediate way with the community. Plus, it could be a fantastic tax write-off if we're able to facilitate a non-profit status." I look to my father. "This would of course require creating another branch of Hitchins altogether, but...I do know a man who would be great for the job."

I do not need to mince words in order for my father to understand my implication. Jeremiah would be brilliant at this work. But for years now, he's missed out on having my brother's talents in the company. There will come a time when he has to step down. I'm ready for that time to be now.

"I'm not dead yet, you know," he says. "I still run this company."

There was a time he would never have spoken in front of our shareholders like this. All that's changed is that we've both gotten older. "I know that, Dad. I'm just not willing to roll over and let you do whatever you want with it. This is a new era at Hitchins." I look to the shareholders. "It can start here and now in this room. You just have to be willing to let it happen."

"This is preposterous!" Dad shouts, slamming his hand on the table and getting to his feet. "This lame attempt at a coup is–it's–"

"This isn't a coup. We're moving in a new direction."

"Axel! This isn't how you make money. The company

needs to make money in order for you to make money. In order for *you all* to make money. We don't have to be reactionary to morality policing."

"We do when people start building lawsuits," one of the investors mentions off-handedly. "What's one park here and there?"

I nod in agreement. These are people who can play with their money like clay. Sure, a park here and there won't hurt them. And that's what I counted on. "Maybe we should bring it to a vote," I say loudly. My voice is commanding and firm, not forced like my father's. He's straining for any inch of control over this room.

This is your room, Axel. Act like it.

"All in favor of repurposing the Seton lot proposal say 'aye', those against, say 'nay'."

It's unprecedented, but every investor around the table says 'aye'. The approval rolls over me like the tide. Until it arrives at my father who is standing next to me. His eyes scan the room, wide and withered. I know he must be wondering how this happened. "Nay," he says softly.

"I'm afraid you've been outvoted," I say. "Could you sit so I can explain the logistical next steps forward?"

My father looks at me, and for the first time in a long time, it breaks my heart. It's the look he would give as he looked at us after Mom died. The look of 'what am I supposed to do with you?' Tired, scared, and so sad. Wishing he could do better. Not knowing how to.

I don't blame him. But I am ready to move on.

Dad sits glumly as I go into the nitty gritty of how we will be moving forward with the park. I tell them about the architect I already have on retainer, outreach possibilities, potential for facility rentals. The conversation is vibrant and exciting. For once, the investors look like they're having a nice time talking about the plans instead of just going through the motions.

When all is said and done, I shake each of their hands as they walk through the door. "Thank you. This is a huge step forward for Hitchins Development."

That leaves me and my father alone in the conference room. He hasn't moved a muscle through my presentation.

However, as soon as we're alone, he gets to his feet, straightens out his jacket, and says, "This is a disappointment."

I watch him as he approaches me. He's never looked older than right now. I wish I could give him a hug. "How so?"

"You think I've worked my whole life for you to tear my company down in a mere hour?"

"*Our* company," I correct. "It's *our* company, isn't it?"

Dad tries to keep his breath steady.

"Dad, I think it's time you retire," I say. "I mean no disrespect to your work and everything you've done to put us in the position we're in now, but it's time you rest. And let me take care of you."

His brow flinches for the briefest moment. As if he might be grateful. That's not the Paul Hitchins way, though. "You don't have what it takes to keep Hitchins afloat. How can you take care of me when you have to declare bankruptcy?"

I don't think my father has ever believed in *me*. He's believed in what he's taught me and the things I've done to try and follow in his footsteps. But he's never believed in what I might be capable of myself. That's why he disowned Jeremiah. He was too far afield of what Dad deemed to be "his" way. After the life Dad has had, I can't blame him for wanting to go the safe route.

"I love you, Dad," I say.

His head jerks back as if I've just slapped him in the face.

"I've never wanted to do anything but make you and Mom proud."

At the mention of my mother, the rims of his eyes go red. "Um…" Dad looks away. "I'll speak with you later." He walks off before he can show even an inch more of emotion.

I sigh, alone in the conference room. That was hard. And yet, I still feel lighter than air. Because Gillian is behind every thought and every word I say. I would not have had the confidence to do this if I hadn't told her the truth of my feelings for her and gotten her in my corner.

She'll be so proud of me. More than that, she'll be so happy. I want nothing more than to make her happy the rest of my life.

My phone starts ringing in my pocket. Lola's calling. I feel my proverbial tail bend between my legs. We still have to tell her. Finding the right time feels impossible. It's certainly not right now. "Hey, sis," I answer.

"What time can I expect you to come pick me up?"

We're meeting Jeremiah for lunch, and I told Lola I'd pick her up from the bakery on my way, so we only had to take one car. I check my watch. "I'm at the Bunker Hill office now. I'll be there in ten."

"A true ten or a businessman ten?"

I hear Gillian giggle in the background and my heart soars. "A true ten. I'm leaving now."

"See you soon!"

We hang up and I hurry out of the office, softly repeating to myself how I'm going to say hello to Gillian so that Lola doesn't suspect a thing.

23

———

GILLIAN

Lola hangs up the phone. "Axel is picking me up in ten."

"Sounds good." In a way, I felt like I was on the phone with Axel too. I could hear his voice through the speaker. It feels wrong to keep lying to Lola like this. And even more wrong that I'm continuing to lie to him. I have to do one thing at a time.

Axel knowing that Stella is his daughter has to come first.

"Okay...I'm going to go check on the bread before I go," Lola says with a sigh. "Need me to do anything before I take off?"

"No, I think I'll be good," I say.

"If you get a minute, the oatmeal cookies should probably be ready to be frosted by the time I'm gone and we need those ready by four."

I make a mental note. "Oatmeal crème pies, got it."

"And if you can restock the beverage cooler, especially–"

"The kombucha. I got it."

Lola giggles to herself. "Silver Lake and its love for kombucha. I don't get it."

"A vegan who doesn't like kombucha. It's a travesty," I say.

"It's just like drinking apple cider vinegar. Blech," she mutters as she disappears into the back.

I scan the bakery. It's lunchtime on a Monday. The bakery is always slow lunchtime on a Monday. It's not until midafternoon that we start seeing an influx of people who need their after-lunch treats. Except for the quiet backing track of Jack Johnson, it's practically silent.

I turn away from the door and grab my phone off the back counter. There's a text from Axel. I always get a head-rush when I see his name on my phone.

> Went well. Can't wait to tell you all about it
> :)

I press the phone to my chest and smile.

Just then, I hear the front door open. I quickly throw my phone back down and greet the customer. "Welcome to Gilly's Vegan Sweets, how can I –" My mouth goes numb at the sight of the customer.

It's not just some stranger from off the street. Not an average Joe.

It's Martin Holtz. He looks just as handsome as he did seven years ago. Same curly brown hair and friendly hazel eyes. Except the expression on his face is not so friendly. "Hello, Gillian."

"Martin. What a surprise."

He smiles. Not kindly. "Is it, though?"

I glance over my shoulder to make sure Lola hasn't overheard. The last thing I need is for her to come rushing in and find out I've been lying all these years about Stella's father before I get a chance to tell Axel the truth. "Martin, what are you doing here?"

"Do you need me to spell it out for you?" he asks with fire in every word.

"N-no. Just...can we do this some other time? Not here?"

"Gillian, you've avoided this conversation for seven years. I'll do it where and when I fucking please."

The vitriol in his voice scrapes across my face. He wasn't a violent or even hot-tempered man. His anger would be justified if what he believes was true.

"You had a *baby*? And you never told me?"

"It's complicated," I say in a low voice. If I can stay on an even keel, maybe he can too. If I could just sit him down over a cup of coffee. We could catch up. I could ask him about his landscaping business and if he was still living with his brother. I could tell him what he needed to know without fear galloping through my entire body.

"Complicated? What's so complicated about a phone call?"

I don't know what to say. All I can do is try to dodge his questions. "If you'd let me explain, then–"

"That's why I came here. To hear you explain."

"Not here."

Martin clenches his fist and approaches the counter. "Here. *Now*."

My heart races. I'm terrified. I'm cornered by my lie, literally.

"If you had my baby and kept her from me..." he trails off and then presses his hands against the counter. "I want a DNA test."

"What for?"

"Because if she's mine–"

"You broke up with me and I was–" *Stop lying, Gillian.* "I promise you, Martin, it won't give you the answers you want."

His jaw drops open. "If she's mine, I want to be a part of her life!"

If Martin was indeed her father, that would be music to my ears. I can only hope when I tell Axel he feels the same.

"Do you know what a mindfuck it is to be a normal guy going through life only to find out on a Saturday night you might have a daughter that you didn't know about?"

"I can only imagine."

"I have a right to know."

I swallow and carefully touch his hands. "Martin...listen to me. I am happy to have this conversation with you. Anytime. Anywhere." I take a deep breath. "But I can't right now."

Martin jerks his hands away from me. "I'm willing to take legal action if I have to."

"Legal action? Martin, please, it's not–"

"I want a paternity test. And if she's mine, I want custody."

I shake my head. This has all gotten so out of hand. "You can't do that."

"Why not? Don't I have a right to get to know my daughter?"

"You don't."

Martin and I go silent and turn toward the source of the voice. Lola has appeared from the back of the bakery.

"What?" Martin asks. I can feel him ready to fight even harder. *Dammit, Lola, why did you have to step in and try and save me?*

Lola holds her head high. "You don't have a right to get to know her because you're not Stella's father." She turns toward me, looks me dead in the eye. Her expression is tender, yet...mysterious. "My brother...Axel. He's Stella's father."

I feel the color drain from my face.

24

AXEL

"Axel. He's Stella's father."

I stop in my tracks, right in the doorway of the bakery.

Did I hear her right? Could my mind be playing tricks on me?

The look on Gillian's face tells me everything I need to know. Her eyes roll toward me, face white as a sheet, her mouth ajar. "Oh no," she whispers.

Lola and Martin turn to look at me as well. Been years since I've seen the guy, but he doesn't look a day over twenty-whatever he was when he and Gillian dated.

Doesn't matter.

I'm still processing what my sister has just said.

I'm Stella's father?

"Is that true?" Martin asks me, eyes hardened.

I open my mouth to speak but nothing comes out.

"Listen, we have some things to talk about, Martin. Family things. Things you shouldn't be privy to since you're not technically a part of this, so…" Lola rambles, coming out from behind the counter and grabbing Martin by the shoulder. "If you'd excuse us–" She marches him up to the door and then looks at me. "We need to talk."

I look back at Gillian. Her eyes are planted on the floor, hands gripping the counter for dear life.

This can't be real. There's no way.

"Excuse me," Martin mumbles.

"Right, sorry," I step aside.

He gives me a sympathetic pat on the shoulder. "Good luck, man."

My body feels as if it's made of straw. You might as well post me up in a field to scare away crows, tie me to a fence post. Otherwise I'm going to blow away. *Is this real life? Does Stella belong to me? Why did Gillian never tell me? Is this all some sort of sick joke?*

Lola closes the door behind Martin, locks the door, and flips the sign to closed.

"How did you know?" Gillian asks in a small voice.

Know. That's a big word. It's not a word where doubt exists. It explains what is true.

I'm Stella's father.

"Gillian, let's sit. Then we can all talk."

"Lola, *how did you know?*"

She looks between the two of us and sighs. "You called me. By accident."

Gillian frowns. "What?"

The desperation in her voice is more than I can bear. It's like she doesn't want me to know and never planned on telling me. I had to find out like this. By accident. My heart breaks.

"You called me by accident! We had just been talking on the phone about planning for the bakery. Must have been lying in bed with your phone out and rolled on it or–" Lola grunts in frustration. "It doesn't matter. All that matters is I heard you talking to yourself. To Stella. Before she was born."

I could have been there. I *should* have been there. Gillian kept it from me.

Or...I guess I kept it from myself. By cutting her out the way I did.

"I picked up because I thought you had something you forgot to mention. And I was yelling at you to hang up the phone, that you were butt dialing me. And then, I heard what you were saying. You were telling her that everything was going to be alright, just the two of you. You didn't need him. You didn't need Axel."

Gillian's face is frozen in horror. I watch her, silently begging for her to look at me.

"That's how I found out."

"Why didn't you say anything?" Gillian asks in the smallest voice.

I can't stop myself from interrupting. "Why didn't *you?*"

Her whole body winces, looking away from me like I've just slammed a door in her face.

Lola touches my arm. "Axel...let's sit. All of us."

She takes me by the arm and leads me over to one of the tables. We both sit and wait for Gillian to unstick herself from her spot. She floats across the room, so silent it's like her feet aren't touching the floor.

I continue to stare at her. Doesn't she owe me that much after all these years? The least she can do after keeping my own child from me. My daughter. The two words in my head feel as heavy as bowling balls and yet make my body feel light and...joyful.

I knew there was something about Stella I couldn't put my finger on. I just never thought it would be *this.*

"Gillian..." Lola begins. Her hand is still on my arm

under the table, steadying me so I don't do something rash. I don't know if I have the energy to lash out at Gillian in anger, no more than I already have. But I know if Lola wasn't grounding me, my entire body would be trembling. "I didn't say anything because I knew you would tell me when you were ready. I just didn't think it would take so long." My sister's lips twist to the side. "If it didn't come out like this, I don't know if you ever would have told me."

"How could I tell you?" Gillian says, her voice thick with emotion. Tears are not far behind, I can tell. "When you made one rule for me and I broke it?"

"You know our friendship would have been stronger than that," Lola replies. "Besides..." She eyes me. "I only didn't want you two to hurt each other."

I shake my head. "Well, look what good that did."

"Do you think I'm an idiot, Axel?" Lola cries out. "Do you think I haven't seen the way you two have looked at each other since Gillian hit puberty? I mean, come on, I'm not a dummy."

Gillian's eyes shoot to me. Now it's my turn to look away. Lola isn't wrong. Gillian was always my kid sister's best friend. I was older, more mature. And then that day when she skinned her knee. From then on, whenever she showed up at the house looking for Lola, she wasn't a kid anymore. She was beautiful. And I'd never been able to look at her the same after that.

I resisted as long as I could.

"Shitting where you eat is a foolish thing to do, that's all," Lola says.

"*Lola*," Gillian scolds. "It wasn't like that!"

"Then what was it like?" Lola asks; there's a glint in her eye. It's a leading question, a question she already knows the answer to.

Gillian's eyes fill with tears. "I had feelings for him. I mean, why would I have had a baby by myself if..." she trails off and looks at me. Now I have the strength not to look away.

Everything hurts. My brain, my heart, every single nerve in my body. I can see how much pain she's in. And I also have to take care of myself. She betrayed me, took away six years of my child's life from me. At the same time, she had my baby because she cared for me so deeply, she couldn't think of another way...even if I didn't deserve it.

How does a man deal with that?

"I know you did, Gill," Lola says with a tender smile. Then, she looks at me. "You did too."

Did? "I *do* have feelings for Gillian. Present tense," I say softly.

Gillian blinks, tears streaking down her face. Part of me wants to dry them. The other part is too hurt to think of helping *her* in this moment.

"You feel that way too?" Lola asks Gillian.

"Why aren't you mad?" Gillian shoots back. "You always said you could never forgive me if something like this happened. You always said–"

"Not *love* Gillian. Not if you *loved* each other."

I do not confirm or deny that I feel this way. It's not a word we've spoken to one another and not one I want someone to speak for me. But I have to wonder, if I didn't love her, would this all be so painful?

"And the second I found out that Stella belonged to my brother..."

"Oh my god," I whisper to myself. It's still sinking in.

"...that's when I knew how you really felt for him. And you–" Lola grabs me by the arm. "You don't care what any woman thinks of you except for Gillian. And me of course, but that's beside the point. She's the only woman you have ever felt the need to defend your character from. I just knew that meant something."

I close my eyes, my jaw tightening. "If you knew, why the hell didn't you say anything? Why didn't you save us all this trouble to–"

"Because you're a fucking grown ass man, Axel!" Lola says firmly. "It's not my job to fight your battles for you. You both needed to grow up and stop putting your pride above your feelings. Don't get me wrong, it's been heartbreaking to watch all these years, especially knowing what I knew, but... better late than never, right?"

If this was just about me and Gillian, yeah. Better late than never. But it's about more than that. It's about my child. Our child.

"I can tell you're upset, Axel," Gillian says. Her face is wet with tears. "So, go ahead. Say what you're feeling."

Lola's hand tightens on me, warning me to be nice. I don't need to punish her. But I need her to see how much this hurts.

Because there's a hole in my heart six years wide I didn't know existed until just now. How can she fill that up?

25

GILLIAN

He looks like a wounded animal who will snap at me if I try to aid in his recovery. And I can't say I blame him. A part of me is heartened that finding out has hurt him. Not because that was my intention (or maybe it was the slightest bit) but because that means he cares enough that missing out on Stella's first years of life feels painful.

"You kept her from me," he says.

"I did."

"And yet you...you dangled her in front of me. For years," Axel says.

"That wasn't my intention," I say. "You were going to be a part of my life regardless because of Lola. It was inevitable you would meet Stella, be around her..."

His brow furrows, eyes trembling. "Gillian, I came to see you in the hospital."

I blink. I think I've blocked that out.

"I...held her. And I didn't know. You didn't tell me."

Axel came with Lola and Jeremiah. I remember fear aching inside me when she told me she was dragging him along. I couldn't fight it if I didn't want to look suspicious.

And neither could he. Now I understand she was trying to put the pieces together for me, right in front of my face. She knew all along and wanted to make sure the bond was created.

I remember how Lola passed her off to Axel. I looked away as long as I could, my heart pounding in my chest. But how could I not just see for a moment if the bond would be so strong he'd recognize her?

Back then, I thought he held her like an alien. Now I know he was just scared. She was so little. And despite that fear, I remember clearly how he smiled. "Last baby I held was you, Lola," he said, cupping Stella's hand in the palm of his hand. "And you immediately started crying."

"Well, she's doing a better job than me, huh?" Lola remarked.

Stella was indeed an angel in his arms. Like she knew. And though he only held her for a minute or so, it was enough.

"Axel, you didn't even want to look at *me*. How could I have come to you to tell you that I was having your baby?"

His body bristles at the words. It's probably still sinking in. "I would have stepped up."

I nearly laugh. "No, you know that's not true."

"How could you say that?" Axel retorts, his voice inflamed with anger.

"Relax..." Lola says and brushes her hand down his arm.

Relax? Maybe he can, but there's no way I can relax. I'm in flight or fight mode. "You don't *know* what you have done, Axel. Hindsight isn't–"

"I would have been there, Gillian. I would have been there for you and for–" His throat locks up. "I would have been there for her. The second I knew."

While he's so terribly emphatic, I know it wouldn't have

gone down like this. We're much older now. So much has happened. He was twenty-five years old. It was a summer fling. He was about to step up at Hitchins. A baby added into the mix would have been the last thing he wanted. "I know for a fact you would have been scared out of your mind and –"

"Of course I would have been scared! But that's–"

"Let her finish, Axel."

Axel seals his lips together and falls back into his seat. For the first time, other than in the grips of passion, he looks messy. His hair is falling out of place, his suit looks rumpled. He looks so small. Like a little boy.

I take a deep breath. I'm getting tired of these revelations, but there's another layer to this he doesn't yet understand. "I thought about telling you. In fact, I was going to."

"Why didn't you?" Axel asks, voice nearly inaudible.

"Because...I heard you talking about your ex. And what she did to you. And I didn't want to be that too."

He frowns at first. He's confused. He doesn't even remember.

"I forget her name. Susie or...Sarah maybe."

"Shelly," he says, hit with a memory he hasn't looked at in god knows how long, maybe years.

"Yeah."

"She wasn't my ex, she was just...a girl. That was, god, that was over a year before us, Gillian."

"It doesn't matter," I say, holding up my hand to stop him. "I don't even know who you were talking to. Some guy. I think he was visiting or–"

"Ugh. Fletch," Lola interrupts. She glares at Axel. "I hate that guy."

Axel narrows his eyes in thought. "He was a college friend. Visiting for the holidays..."

"Right. I heard you two talking. Out on the deck. About Shelly. You were telling him how she tried to entrap you into having a baby with her. Poked holes in the condoms, said she was on the pill and wasn't. It was clear you were very relieved to not be dealing with that, so–"

"A baby with a woman I barely knew is a completely different story than a baby with you, Gillian, you have to know that."

I shake my head. "That wasn't all of it. You were saying just awful things about her. Calling her names and–things I don't like to repeat."

His face falls.

"I'm not saying she wasn't a bad person. Or that you didn't deserve your anger. I'd just never heard you talk like that. Even when we teased each other. You never used words like that."

"I don't anymore. I was young, Gillian. You have to–"

"I had just found out I was having a girl, Axel," I go on, eyes filling again with tears. "Besides, you wouldn't even look at me, acknowledge my existence. I was already tearing myself inside, forcing myself to go to you and going through the humiliation of asking for your attention to tell you something hard, and then hearing that? How could I in good conscience invite her father into her life when he spoke about women like that?"

Axel's mouth droops open. "You could have told me the other night."

My eyes widen.

"You *should* have told me the other night, Gillian," he says with a firm nod. "I know I said shitty things when I was younger. I don't have an excuse. But I've grown up now. I'm trying to step up. I made it clear to you that Stella is not a problem to me. She's a part of you. That I want."

I don't know what to say. There are a million things I *could* say but all of them would pale in comparison to the hurt I've caused him.

"I didn't deserve to know? Still?"

I swallow. "Of course you did. I'm sorry. I was...scared."

We are all silent for a long time.

Abruptly, Axel pushes himself up from his chair. "I have to go."

My body surges to follow him as he heads toward the door. "Wait–" I grab his arm.

He continues to pull away. "I need time to think, Gillian."

"But –"

"Please, I can't–"

"We've already lost so much time, Axel," I say tearfully. "Can't we sit and..." I lose my ability to speak when I see how his green eyes are filled with an indescribably amount of pain. The pain I've caused him, the pain he's helped caused himself.

Together, we have created quite the mess. And god, does it hurt.

"I just need some time to think, alright?"

If it weren't for Lola's hand sliding onto my shoulder, I'd never let go. If I let him walk away, who is to say he'll ever come back? "Let him go, Gillian. It's okay."

I release his arm and step back. As soon as he's free to leave, he disappears through the door. My legs give out and I drop to the floor, crying more tears than I know what to do with. How could I have let this happen? Why did I wait so long? Why did I take him away from her? Away from us.

More importantly, why did I keep the thing Stella wants most from her for so long?

Lola sinks down to the ground with me and wraps her arms around me. "Shhh...Honey, it's okay."

"What's wrong with me?" I weep.

She pulls me into her chest. "Nothing. He just needs time to cool off. It's alright. It's alright."

I cry it all out on her shoulder. Don't know how long I'm there, but when I'm done, my face hurts all over. "I'm so stupid."

"Don't talk about my friend like that," Lola says, wiping my cheeks clean of tears. "You're not stupid. You were scared. That's okay. So was he."

I stare at my friend. "How did you know all this time? How didn't you say anything?"

Lola looks away. "It's the hardest thing I've ever done. But...I've gotten to be in Stella's life every step of the way. I thought that would be enough until you were ready."

I smile with the last bit of strength I have in my face and embrace her. "It was, Lola. It really was." Stella has had a Hitchins in her life from day one. And I'll always be grateful for it.

"He'll come around, Gillian. He will. I know he's got that hard exterior, but all Axel has ever wanted is to be chosen."

I can choose him. That will be easy.

"As soon as you do that...as soon as you let him in..." Lola's voice warbles. "He's going to be the best dad. I just know it."

THE NEXT FEW days are the hardest and most painful not hearing from Axel. I had him and then I lost him. Seems to be the story of my life. I have to act as if everything is normal, which makes it all that much more difficult.

On top of running the bakery and taking care of Stella, I have to be a pseudo party planner as Harley's courthouse wedding and reception are coming up this weekend. The back of the bakery has become an assembly line of various sweets and treats. Lola and I decided to close the bakery on Friday so that we can focus on getting everything done for the wedding.

I have to remain steadfast in getting it all done for Harley. From the moment I found out she was expecting, I have been her rock. And I'm not going to let myself falter in that role.

However, in the back of my mind, I'm always thinking about Axel.

Not to mention another intrusive thought as well.

I've decided that Martin is owed an explanation. An in person one. Not just a text or a phone call. I've made his world topsy turvy and that deserves attention and apology. So, I reach out to him. His number is still the same. I just have to unblock it. I promise him that I can clear everything up if he'll just give me a few minutes of his time.

We schedule coffee for Saturday morning, an hour and change before Harley's ceremony. I've been telling myself it's just better to get it over with. One last thing on my mind. I want to have all my ducks in a row for when I see Axel again. And Lola has promised me he will still be attending Harley's reception. Martin will be a distant memory by that point.

I just have to deal with him.

So, here I sit, at an Alfred Coffee in Beverly Hills, wearing a dress that's a little too fancy for a Saturday morning coffee.

Martin walks in looking like a meerkat on hind legs, alert and nervous. I wave him down. "Martin!"

When he sees me, his eyes widen. "Didn't realize this was a black-tie occasion," he says, putting his hands into his linen pants.

I chuckle and adjust the bodice of my dress. "I have plans after this. You're not underdressed. I promise. I, um..." I gesture to the coffee in front of his chair. "Got you a coffee."

Martin looks at it as he sits carefully. "Thank you."

"So...I guess, let me cut right to the chase. You're not Stella's father."

He frowns. "Hm. How am I supposed to believe that?"

"I knew you'd say that," I say with a smile. We did spend enough time together for me to know him well. And Martin is a skeptical guy. He isn't just going to take my word for it. I reach into my purse and pull out Stella's birth certificate. "Stella was born in May the year after we broke up. There's no way given the timeline that you could have been her father."

Martin takes the certificate and scrutinizes it.

"I promise, it's the real deal."

He nods slowly and lets out a sigh of relief. "Okay. I believe you."

"But I didn't bring you all the way out here just for that."

Martin lifts his gaze to mine.

"I owe you an apology," I say. *Deep breath, Gillian. It's not about your relationship in the past. It's about what's happened now.* "I shouldn't have made you the scapegoat. That wasn't fair. It was unnecessarily cruel to put you through this. I never thought you'd find out; it just was easier than–"

"It's okay."

I stop and give him a smile.

"I mean, I appreciate your apology. I'm just more relieved than anything."

I burst into laughter and he laughs too. "Sorry, that's so funny."

"Don't get me wrong," he says with a smile. "If she was mine, I'd want to be a part of her life. But I'm still figuring out my own, so..."

It's funny. That's how I felt when I found out I was pregnant. How can I invite a life into mine when it's on such unsteady ground? And yet...Stella is what made me figure everything out. A child is something you can never be ready for. But when it happens, you get ready. And make it work. "Well, I'm glad to bring you some relief."

Martin nods. "Well, it's good to see you, Gillian. Now that the smoke has cleared."

"You too."

We chat for a little bit longer, doing a generic catch-up. I've got one eye on the door the whole time, thinking about my drive over to the courthouse. When we part ways, we actually give each other an amicable hug. It couldn't have gone better if I'd written a script for it.

However, I don't have much time to dwell. I've got a wedding to get to.

***

My sisters and I are squeezed into the first row of the courtroom on one side while Dad and Victoria, Grant's little sister, are on the other. I've got Stella balanced neatly on my lap and tiny Tana is strapped to Dad's chest in a sling, sleeping through her parents' wedding.

Harley looks immaculate. The black dress was absolutely the way to go. Amy and Dana did an amazing job getting her ready. And Grant doesn't look too shabby either.

Between them stands the judge, a very thin and gaunt older man with a friendly smile, his robes hanging off of him. "Grant, do you take this woman to be your wife, to live together in holy matrimony..." The judge barely starts the traditional vows and I'm already in tears.

"Mommy, why are you crying?" Stella asks, cupping her hand around my neck. "Are you sad?"

I smile. "Not sad at all." I glance over at Dad who also has started crying. Victoria takes his hand tightly and hands him a tissue. "We are crying because it's beautiful."

"I do," Grant says. His voice is strained with emotion, blue eyes swimming as he admires every inch of Harley's face.

The judge begins to recite the vows for Harley too, but Stella is still curious. "I don't feel like crying."

"That's okay, sweetie," I say and kiss the top of her head. "Sometimes happy things don't have to make you cry." Inside though, I know she'll understand when she's older. Life can be so hard, that pure moments like this where the world stops and acknowledges how beautiful love can be are cause for tears.

"I do," Harley says, a tear loosening from the corner of her eyes.

Grant swipes it away immediately and cups her cheek.

God, I want love like that. I thought I almost had it with Axel. Maybe I still can.

Grant and Harley exchange their rings and the room holds its breath as the judge lifts his head proudly. This must be his favorite part. "By virtue of the authority vested in me under the laws of the State of California–"

My sisters and I all grab hands.

"I now pronounce you husband and wife." He looks at Grant. "You may kiss the–"

Before he can finish, Harley launches herself into Grant's arms and kisses him with all her might. We erupt into cheers and applause. Tana doesn't even stir, even when Grant and Harley immediately rush over to collect her from Dad, embracing her for the first time as husband and wife.

"Mommy?" Stella asks in a quivering voice. She looks up at me. Axel's eyes swimming with tears. "I think I get why people cry when they're happy now."

"Oh, my little one...oh, my sweet little girl," I coo to her, pulling her close and kissing her. I can only pray that her tears do not come from seeing a life that isn't like hers. A mother, a father, a baby...all together.

Hold on, Stella, I think as I rock her back and forth. *Mommy's going to fix everything.*

26

AXEL

I CONTEMPLATED NOT COMING AT ALL, BUT I KNOW I'D never hear the end of it from Lola and Jeremiah. So, I settled on being fashionably late.

It's hard to believe that I'm inside a big movie studio when it really feels like I'm walking a carnival midway at twilight. There's a Ferris wheel and carousel, incredible amounts of fried food, and games complete with prizes. The only thing that confirms that I'm not outside is the air conditioning and the occasional studio lights I spot up above.

When I emerge from the "midway", that's when it really seems like a wedding reception. People are dancing to the music while guests mill and seethe in riotous conversation. I immediately spot Harley and Grant bouncing baby Tana back and forth. She's gotten so big so quickly. Of course Harley's wearing a black dress. Quintessential her going against the grain. I should go congratulate them, but I'm too nervous. I feel like I might throw up.

I run my hand through my hair and scan the party for Lola. Need her to calm my nerves before I –

"Axel!"

Oh no. That little voice. I know it so well. In fact, it's been playing in my dreams.

Stella runs up to me, holding a half-eaten cone of cotton candy. "Hi!"

"Hey, kiddo. Look at that cotton candy, huh?"

She jumps up on her toes and leans forward, almost like she's going to hug me. I don't think I'd be able to handle that. I'd burst into tears. Luckily (yet disappointingly), she doesn't. "You want some?" She holds the cotton candy up toward me.

"You know, I'm actually good for now. Maybe later."

Stella smiles at me; it sends a shock through my body. Her little green eyes, my eyes, looking up at me with all the sweetness in the world. How did I never notice it before?

"Hitchins!"

I look up and see Hunter Ricks waving over at me. His daughter, Jessica, is hidden behind his pant leg.

Hunter moved in on the other side of the Solace's a little over a year ago now. He's the complete opposite of me in terms of looks. Strapping with long hair and a full beard. I wanted to hate the guy at first, but he's just so goddamn nice and easygoing. He runs the Ricks Group, a hotel conglomerate. I can't even imagine how deep his pockets are.

Stella immediately leaps to attention and rushes over to Hunter where she greets Jessica with an outstretched hand. The shy little girl takes it without hesitation, and they begin to play some sort of game where they dance in circles and leap in the air.

It pulls at my heartstrings to see what a good kid Stella is. Hurts to know I had literally nothing to do with it. And yet, I'm proud that she's so kindhearted.

I have Gillian to thank for that...even though my heart

still aches she didn't deem me worthy enough to tell me about Stella until she was forced to.

I follow in Stella's wake. Hunter greets me with a hearty handshake. "Good to see you, man."

"You too," I say. "This is wild, isn't it?"

"A little overkill for my taste, but..."

I laugh. "Says the guy who boasts a hotel with a solid gold bathtub."

"Whoa. That was *not* my idea," Hunter replies.

Jessica lets out a squeal as Stella chases her. Their smiles are so big I'm afraid their faces might get stuck that way.

"But the girls are having fun, so that's all that matters."

"Yeah..." I'm tempted for a moment to ask where Gillian is, but not sure if my heart can handle it yet.

"So, I heard about the movement on your property development at Seton. I think that's a good move," Hunter says with a smile.

I can't even describe how nice it feels for him to say that. "Thank you."

"But be honest with me about something. Did your old man really agree to that?"

I open my mouth and then close it.

He bursts out laughing.

"Is it that obvious?"

Hunter puts his hands in his pockets. "I've just been in your shoes almost exactly. I know how hard it can be to work with your dad."

I eye Hunter. He's never mentioned his father, at least not to me. I always figured it was some sort of trauma. After all, the death of Harold and Penelope Ricks was national news.

"It's hard to step out from their shadow. Even if they're

no longer around," Hunter says, his face going slack toward the end of his sentence. "Anyway, you have an ally in me."

I nod. "Thanks, Ricks."

"It was a smart move. Maybe not a moneymaking one, but a good one."

"That's true...gonna have to start picking up the slack a little on the project front I think."

"Well, I might have something for you, then."

I raise an eyebrow. "Really?"

"The group is talking about expanding into the more family friendly hotel ventures. You know, think small scale Disney resorts but with a more outdoor activity focus. We're just having trouble finding the right locations for the right prices and..." Hunter trails off and gestures to me. "That's where you would come in."

My smile broadens. "I think I definitely have some ideas when it comes to that."

"Knew you would," he says with a firm nod. Hunter glances over at Jessica and Stella who have dropped to their bottoms and started sharing the cotton candy. The smile on his face is so placid and warm.

I want that. That feeling. I don't want to look at Stella and be scared. Even if Gillian and I can't figure things out (dear god, I hope we can), she's mine. I want her to feel that. "She's a cute kid," I say with a nod toward Jessica.

"Thanks," he says. "I wish she wasn't so shy, but...she's still little. Gotta be patient."

"That must be hard. Patience."

Hunter chuckles. "You know, I actually find that because my working life moves so fast, it's easy to slow down with Jessica. Kind of like a yin and a yang."

"That's pretty impressive. Especially since you're doing it on your own."

His eyebrows jump.

"Sorry, don't mean to–" *Damn, why do you have to go pointing out the obvious?* "It's just impressive. I don't know a lot of guys who could do that."

Hunter hums thoughtfully. "I just don't think many of them are put in positions where they have to step up and be the only one. You'd be surprised how the instincts kick in when the time comes."

We watch the girls for a few moments as they lay back on the ground and stick their feet in the air, clicking their dress shoes together.

It's crazy, but I already feel that instinct. That's my little girl. I've got a job to do. Protect her. Take care of her. Make sure she feels the love I have for her. But I missed those first years. Six of them. How would she feel if I had been around all this time? How will she feel that I'll be around now? Perhaps I'm in over my head. I have a game of catch up to do that I'm not sure I'll ever win.

"You got any words of wisdom?" I ask.

Hunter gives me a sidelong glance. "Getting baby fever, Hitchins?"

"I mean, gotta...gotta have a woman for that, don't I?" I say, my voice faltering with the distant lie that not only might I already have a woman, but I already have the child too.

"It's never a bad thing to know what you want."

I don't respond. My eyes are glued to Stella as she sits up and rests her hands on her knees. She looks around the room with her attentive green eyes, a small pert smile on her lips. Watching the world. Just like Gillian. And a little bit of me somewhere in there, maybe. My heart thumps in my chest.

"Be patient. Remember all the joyful moments. When

they cry, just remember they won't always be so little or need you so much. That always hits me right in the chest when I see how fast Jess is growing up."

Stella gets up and then holds her hand out to help Jessica. My eyes are feeling misty.

"But my biggest piece of advice is..." Hunter sighs. "This is a 'do as I say, not as I do,' kind of thing, so you just have to take my word for it."

I nod. "I will."

Hunter swallows thickly. "Find someone who is always in your corner. Who will fight for your family before anything else."

I can hear the pain in his voice. "You mean..."

Hunter grimaces. "Jessica is the best thing that has ever happened to me. And I have no regrets. But I wish she had a mother that could put her above everything else. Even before me. Someone who I could go to whose priority is also my little girl. Our family. Because when you create something so precious...I mean, I want to protect that little girl with my whole life. If it had to be me or her, I'd go first. You get what I'm saying?"

The heaviness of what he's saying is juxtaposed against the image of little girls laughing and whispering to each other. I have a lot to learn about Stella. A lot of time to make up for. And yet, I can feel what he's saying deep in my bones.

"You can ask Gillian too, I'm sure she'd say the same thing," he says with a subtle smile and a nod across the room.

I follow his gaze. Through the throngs of excited party guests, my eyes lock on Gillian. And my god, does she look beautiful in a burnt red dress covered in dark flowers, wrapped in a shawl. Her hair falls in waves down her shoulders. She's listening intently to Amy who is gesticulating wildly. Not sure if it's something good or bad from the expression on her face.

She must feel me looking at her because, suddenly, Gillian's eyes snap to mine. The entire world drifts away when I see her relieved smile creep up onto her face.

I feel a little hand slide into mine and look down to see Stella beside me. She smiles up at me and tugs on my hand. "Come say hi."

It's like she knows somehow. I guess it's true what they say about kids: they know way more than you give them credit for.

"Thanks, Hunter," I say over my shoulder.

"Any time," he replies.

Stella leads me across the room toward Gillian, and thank god for that because I can't see a damned thing. I'm too caught up in the feeling of her little hand in mine, so unfalteringly gentle. It's like she knows. But there's no way, right?

As I approach Gillian with Stella's hand in mine–no. With *our daughter's* hand in mine, I haven't ever felt like more of a man in all my life.

"Mommy, look who I found!" Stela cries out as we get closer. "Axel!"

She doesn't even know how my name chafes against my skin. It's not what I should have ever been to her. And I'm determined to make sure I change that as soon as possible.

Gillian nods. "I see that, Stella. Are you making sure he's having fun?"

"Are you having fun?" Stella asks covertly.

I laugh. "A much better time now, I think."

My eyes meet Gillian's for a prolonged moment.

"Stella!" Amy cries out. "It's time for a ride on the carousel."

"I already rode the carousel, Auntie Amy."

Amy scoops her away from me. "What child doesn't want to ride a carousel? Come on!" They hightail it out of here, arguing back and forth, Stella looking back at us until we're out of her sight.

I turn back to Gillian. "Um...hi."

"Hi," she replies. "Glad you made it."

"Of course, of course. You look...nice." *You idiot. She looks way better than nice.*

"Thank you."

We blink at each other.

"I promise you she doesn't know yet, she's just...perceptive maybe," Gillian says.

My mouth is dry. I don't know what to say.

"Do you want to grab a drink and maybe talk?" she offers.

"I'd like nothing more."

Gillian giggles. "Good."

Once I get a little bit of liquid courage in me, I'll be able to say what I need to say. By the end of the night, Gillian will know where I stand and how much I need our family to be whole.

27

______

GILLIAN

It's extremely hard to find some peace and quiet at a reception such as this one. But after grabbing two signature cocktails (Harley's favorite, an Old Fashioned with three cherries), practically downing them in one go, then wandering around, Axel and I decide to rip off the band-aid and head toward the only place two people can really be alone: the Ferris wheel.

We climb on with the assistance of the ride operator, sitting side by side on the small bench. Being next to Axel is intoxicating. I can smell him, his cologne of amber and spice and something just him. It's divine. Reminds me how nice it is to be near him.

The ride sighs under us as our bench is lifted into the sky, higher and higher. I clutch the bar in front of me nervously. Thank god for the Old Fashioned. It's giving me the courage to say what I need to, even if it's making my stomach flip flop more than it usually would on a ride like this.

"Well, I guess I'll start," I say. My meeting with Martin has already primed me for my vulnerability. Good practice for something way more important. "I owe you an apology. For keeping Stella from you."

Axel's face tightens. "It's okay, Gillian."

"No, it's not. I stole what could have been something amazing from all of us."

"There's no use harping on what could have been any longer."

I shake my head. "How can I stop when I've done something so horrible?"

"Gillian, don't talk about it like that." Axel grabs my hand, massaging it tenderly. "You were protecting yourself. I'm only sorry you felt you had to protect yourself from me."

The Ferris wheel reaches its zenith and then groans to a stop. From here we can see the entirety of the party. Though below it is as rollicking as a true carnival, up here it is quiet. Almost breezy. If not for the hot studio light pointed at us.

"I wasn't protecting myself. I was trying to hurt you," I murmur, casting my eyes down into my lap.

"How could you be hurting me if you never thought you'd tell me, huh?" he replies in a soft voice.

It reaches inside me and tugs at my heartstrings, reminds me of all the times his voice has been just for me. He's letting me hear it again. That must mean something good, right?

"Hey, chin up," he whispers and brushes his knuckle against the underside of my chin.

I raise my eyes to his, blinded by the most beautiful green. Axel has never looked so good. His dark hair coiffed so casually. The collar of his shirt framing his pale neck. The thin tie resting on his dress shirt. I could have him right here if the whole world wasn't below us.

"I would rather have the rest of our lives together, the

three of us, than the past six years and never have us be together."

Though that warms me from the inside out, I shake my head. "It didn't have to be like that."

"I was such an idiot back then, Gillian. I don't even know if I would have been able to appreciate how wonderful I had it with you if we had been brought together then." He sighs and then pushes a lock of hair off of my face, fingertips grazing my skin. "I'd like to think I would have, but there's no way to know."

I rest my cheek in his hand.

"But I'm here now."

"Axel..."

"You have done an incredible job raising Stella. All on your own, too. I'm terrified all I'll do is get in the way and mess her up."

I grab the lapels of his jacket. "You won't. I promise you won't."

"You don't know that."

"Yes, I do. I do know it."

His eyes widen and the corners of his mouth lift.

"You might not believe it, but I do. Beyond a shadow of a doubt." I press my hands to his chest. "She needs you. *I* need you."

Axel beams. "I need you both too."

I gasp happily, contentment spread across my face.

"I know it'll take work, but I'm willing to do whatever it takes to give us a fair shake, Gillian."

"Me too."

The Ferris wheel lurches forward again. It doesn't matter. I'm trapped in his gaze. "You're the strongest woman I've ever met," Axel whispers.

For some reason, that's the thing that pushes me over the edge. I close the gap between us, planting my lips on his. Axel pulls me into his chest as if we could somehow be even closer. It feels like one of those old Hollywood kisses. Deep, necessary, unyielding. Because it *is* all those things. We have pushed each other away for so long that this inevitable coming back together is an explosion.

I need Axel. I need to know if we can do this.

Because I really believe that we can.

Our kiss is interrupted by whoops and hollers. We break apart, noticing that the Ferris wheel is slowing to a stop at the bottom and a bunch of our family and friends are standing around, reveling in our happiness.

Axel helps me off the Ferris wheel and we are met with hugs and kisses. My sisters all crowd around me, namely Harley, who looks completely dazed. "Why didn't you tell me?"

"Trust me, Harley, I wouldn't have even known what to say," I exclaim. I've a lot of explaining to do but my sisters need to be sitting down for that one.

I'm passed off to my dad who is eyeing me with playful suspicion. "What?" I ask.

"Nothing, just...hm. I knew there was something you weren't telling me," he says and then glances over at Stella.

I punch him on the shoulder. "You don't know anything."

"I'm your dad, Gillian." He wraps his arm around me and kisses my cheek. "I know everything."

Axel and I meet again after being passed around from person to person. We look at each other with breathless smiles. "That was quite the reception, huh?" he asks.

"You could say that again."

"Hey you two."

We both turn to find Lola, Stella beside her, holding her hand. The two most important people in all of this, really. Stella is bashfully teetering from foot to foot, smiling in a way I've never had the privilege of seeing.

"Someone has a request for you," Lola says, holding up Stella's hand.

I step forward and get down on my knees, holding my arms out to her. "Are you confused, honey?"

"Go ahead," Lola encourages Stella.

Stella comes toward me and nods. "A little." She takes my hands, looking down at the ground, nibbling on her lower lip. "But it's okay."

I grin. "You're so brave, Stella." *I wish you never had to be.* "Can we explain it to you?"

"Maybe later," she says, mouth twitching into a smile. "Can we dance now instead?"

I frown and start to respond until I hear a familiar song playing.

"Those fingers in my hair...that sly come-hither stare..."

My jaw falls ajar.

"All three of us, please," Stella says, grabbing for one of Axel's hands.

Both of us are dumbfounded as she pulls us out onto the dance floor, but the second our eyes meet, we start to laugh.

"That strips my conscience bare, it's witchcraft..."

"How are we going to do this, Stella, huh?" Axel asks as we stand in a circle, our hands linked together.

Stella looks between us as if that will answer the question.

"And I've got no defense for it."

"I've got an idea," Axel says, eyeing me.

"The heat is too intense for it."

Without warning, he lifts Stella off the ground and puts her on his hip. She laughs. "Is this okay?"

Our little girl nods. With one arm wrapped around Axel's shoulder, she reaches out to me.

And so does he. Together, they pull me close into our strange little dance. It's not so strange, though. It's perfect. Because I have the most beautiful pairs of green eyes looking back at me as we sway around the floor.

I'm transported back in time to that summer when everything changed. I was finishing up pastry school and Axel was overworked by his father. We started unwinding together after our long days. Wine, music. And suddenly, we were spending every night together.

Until finally that Frank Sinatra song put a spell over us, and we fell into each other's arms.

Now, here we are again.

"Cause it's witchcraft...wicked witchcraft..."

Yes, it really is some sort of witchcraft. Here Axel and I are, with our daughter between us. I Never thought I'd have this.

"Are those happy tears, Mommy?" Stella asks, touching my face.

I smile and nod. *God, all you do is cry, Gillian? Can't you stop that for just one second?* "Very happy."

Stella turns to look at Axel. "Kiss her, would you?"

Axel grins. "Gladly." He kisses my cheek tenderly, his nose lingering against my skin.

"On the lips, silly!"

Axel and I both laugh. "You heard the woman! Lips it is," Axel replies and then kisses me again.

I wrap my arms tighter around both of them, lost in his lips while Stella giddily squeals. The song swells around us, carrying us across the floor, into the next step of this adventure.

I never thought my love story would look like this. After Axel, I never thought I'd even get one.

But now that it's happening, I can't imagine a story more perfect than this.

28

AXEL

I scrape the remains of the burnt, inedible lasagna into the trash can, trying to ignore my skyrocketing pulse. The smoke is just clearing from the kitchen, but I can still smell the acridity of vegan cheese burning on the bottom of the oven.

I'm no chef, but I thought I could at least follow a recipe for once in my life. I wanted to make this night as special as possible.

Then, to my horror, the doorbell rings. I check my watch. *Fuck.* Gillian and Stella are early. Like way early. I tear off my apron that hasn't seen a day of wear in its life until today and rush through the house, checking all the nooks and crannies.

My house is that of a bachelor in an LA way, which is to say it's pretty bland. It's a modern bungalow I designed myself, all steel and glass. All the decorations were chosen by an interior designer without much thought or care from me.

The only color is a bountiful bouquet of pink, orange, and white flowers that I had sent over for Gillian.

The doorbell rings again and Stella's little voice shouts, "Hellooooo?" followed by Gillian shushing her quickly.

I smooth my hand down the front of my white dress shirt. *Now or never, Axel.* And, obviously, at this point, I'm choosing now.

I open the bulky mahogany door as quickly as its weight will allow me. My breath immediately leaves my chest when my eyes land on Gillian. She's smiling her gorgeous smile that I've known for so many years, wearing a green button up dress with a floral pattern. Her blonde hair is pinned back out of her face with a few bobby pins. "Hi," I say, unable to find more words than that.

"Are you okay?" she asks. "You look frazzled."

"N-no. I'm fine. I'm..." I'll explain everything later. For now, I just want to hold her. I wrap my arms around her and give her a kiss on the cheek.

We've seen each other enough over the past couple weeks that this action is easy. Our bodies are starting to remember each other, get used to our closeness. Consequently, it feels so easy.

Things between Gillian and me are amazing. We've fallen into a relationship quickly and without fear. Though both of us have busy schedules, we try to fit each other in whenever possible.

"*Ahem.*"

I break away from Gillian and look down at Stella. "Sorry, kiddo, didn't see you there."

She frowns and puts her hands on her hips. "I picked out this dress just for tonight!"

I get down on a knee at her eye level. Still feeling so familiar, yet so odd, to see my own eyes reflected back at me, especially surrounded by so many features I attribute to Gillian. "Forgive me, Stella. Give me a twirl, will you?"

Stella's frown turns upside down and she spins around, the light blue dress flowing in a circle around her. "Do you see?" she asks, showing me the fabric patterned with cream-colored stars. "Stars! Because my name means star. Did you know that?"

I can't help but smile at my little girl. Stella still doesn't know that I'm her daddy. That's why Gillian brought her here tonight. We've decided it's time to tell her the truth.

We wanted to tell her as soon as possible, but we were still navigating the start of our relationship and we wanted a semblance of security and answers for any questions she might have, so we decided to wait for a little bit to see in which capacity I would be in her life, as a part of the household or as a co parent, no other option was ever on the table. Now that I knew who she was to me, I'd never be without her again.

It also helped her to get used to having me around all the time.

Now the time has come. We know that what's between us is real and deep, and we can invite Stella fully into it. Let our family start for real. "You know, your mother *may* have mentioned that to me..."

Stella frowns again and looks at Gillian. "Mommy, that's *my* fun fact."

"Don't be mad at your mother. I asked," I say. Which is sort of the truth. I guessed on my own and had Gillian confirm it. She'll understand why soon enough.

"It smells like...burning?" Gillian says, sniffing the air.

I remember the burnt lasagna and get back to my feet. "Uh, yeah. That. Funny story..."

Gillian smirks. "Alright."

"I wanted to make you girls a special dinner, but I don't cook very often and –'"

"Let me guess," Stella says, crossing her arms. "You burnt it."

Gillian and I laugh. I nod. "You got it, kiddo." Then, I sheepishly look back at Gillian. "So...dinner is in the trash."

She giggles and pats my chest. "Don't worry, honey. That's what ordering in is for."

"I know, I just wanted this to be...a special night. It's a big night to have my two favorite girls in my house for the first time," I say.

Stella reaches up and reaches up to pat my chest too. "It's okay. We'll get In-N-Out."

<hr>

It turns out In-N-Out eaten on the patio at twilight was exactly what we needed. The three of us sit around the table, eating and chatting the night away.

Just like everything with Gillian, things feel easy with Stella too. She's so personable for someone her age, seemingly unfettered by shyness or nerves. The conversation is equal parts all of us. Or should I say it's mostly Gillian and Stella. My heart is still pounding, burnt dinner notwithstanding.

After all, it's a big night for us.

Gillian and I went through the order of events several times in the days leading up to today. She promised me softly over and over that it would all be okay. "The only thing Stella has ever wanted that I haven't been able to give her is her father. There's no reason to be scared."

There are still moments I feel hurt that Gillian kept me away. Who knows how close Stella and I could be now if I had been her father right from the beginning? However, I have to remain grateful I get this opportunity at all. That Gillian and I finally put our egos aside to find each other.

Better late than never. I guess Lola was right about that after all.

Stella takes the last sip of her milkshake and sighs happily. "Mm. So good."

"That was a lot of dairy," Gillian remarks, picking up the empty cup.

"Relax," I tell her, touching her knee gently under the table. "It's a special occasion."

Gillian's warm brown eyes meet mine. There's something tentative in her gaze. She's nervous too. Every step of this journey, she's been my rock, assuring me that our daughter will have nothing but open arms for me. I never thought she'd be nervous too. After all, she knows Stella better than I do. At least for now.

"I have a gift for you, Stella," I declare.

"Oh! Really?" she asks, vibrating excitedly in her seat.

"Mhm. Just a small thing." I reach into my pocket and pull out a small, flat jewelry box. The gift was my idea, but I wanted to clear it with Gillian first. She burst into tears when I told her. Her heart is so achingly full of love for Stella. I can't believe how lucky I am that she chose to have my child, even when I didn't deserve it.

Gillian takes Stella's hand. "Why don't you come over here and stand in front of Axel so he can give it to you?"

Stella cautiously approaches me, eyeing Gillian. She's a smart kid. She knows something is up.

Once she's standing right before me, I put the box down on the table. "Would you like to open it?"

She smiles and nods.

"Go ahead."

Stella lifts the lid of the box and gasps. "A star!"

Inside is a necklace with a tiny gold star hanging from the chain. I picked it out myself.

"Like my name!" she giggles, beaming at me.

I nod. "Exactly. I wanted to get you something that could always be a symbol of how much I care about you. I know it might be a little weird that your mom has this new guy around all the time. But just as much as I'm her new guy, I'm yours too. I hope that as we get closer, you can start to feel me in your heart the way I already..." *Don't cry... don't cry.* "The way I already feel you in mine."

Stella smiles hard, her shoulders going up to her ears.

My eyes flick to Gillian briefly. She's holding it together really well, leaning on her hand and admiring a scene I bet she's pictured in her head so many times as a faraway fantasy. "Can I put it on you?"

"Yes, please."

"Turn around for me, then."

Stella turns around per my instruction. I take the delicate necklace out of the box and dangle it out in front of her face. Gillian pulls Stella's hair out of the way so I can put it around her neck. "It's a little long," I say as I clasp it. "But you can grow into it."

"I can wear it forever!" Stella remarks excitedly, looking to Gillian.

Gillian nods. "You can." She touches Stella's shoulders. This is her moment to shine. "You like Axel, don't you?"

"Yes, a lot," Stella says, looking down at the small star and then back at me. I touch her shoulder gently, feel my heart swell with pride. *My little girl...*

"Good. I like him a lot too," Gillian replies. "There's something that we need to tell you, Stella."

Stella is quiet, waiting.

Gillian swallows. Our eyes meet for just a moment, but

in that moment, I send her a message. *You can do it.* She takes Stella's hands. "Axel is your daddy, honey. Your real, *real* daddy."

Stella is silent. The whole world is silent. I hold my breath, waiting to hear what she has to say. What if she bursts into tears? Hurt that I've just now shown up in her life this way? Or what if she's mad? What if she never really wanted a dad in the first place? So many what ifs that could break my heart.

However, I should know better when it comes to Stella. She turns around and looks into my face with curiosity. Eyes perusing every one of my features.

I feel my eyes prick with tears. This is the first time my daughter is seeing me as her father. Like we should have met six years ago in the hospital. I should have gotten to hold her right away. She would have remembered my voice from the womb and would already know how I say, "I love you."

This isn't how it goes traditionally. But this is the beginning of our story.

Carefully, Stella touches my cheek. Her curiosity melts into a knowing smile. I can't possibly comprehend how, but it's almost like she knew all along, was just waiting for us to catch up. "Hi, Daddy."

I can't hold back my tears, though I'm smiling at the same time. "Hi, baby."

Without warning, she wraps her arms around my neck and buries herself into my chest. It's not like it's the first time. It's like...I've just been gone a few weeks and she's welcoming me back home. I hold her to me with all of my might, pulling her onto my lap and cradling her in my arms.

Eventually, we're all crying. Stella into my shoulder, me into her hair, Gillian into her hands. I reach out and pull

Gillian toward us. She gets on her knees behind Stella, embracing the both of us.

Stella draws away, face decorated with crystals of tears. "Daddy?"

I won't ever get tired of hearing her say that. I run my hand through her hair. "What is it, Stella?"

"I think I..." She blinks, more tears rushing down her cheeks. "I think I love you."

I grin the proudest, happiest grin I've ever had. "Oh, Stella, I think I love you too."

Gillian's hands clutch my waist harder. I cup the back of her head as our eyes meet. In that one look, I know we have years and years of more 'I love yous' ahead of us. Even if we haven't said it to each other, I know it's there.

Now, I just need to tell her too.

***

By the end of the evening, I offer to take my girls home. I need to make up for as much lost time as possible, so every second I get with them is worth its weight in gold.

Stella doesn't seem to be getting tired. She talks the whole way home, telling me anything and everything she can think of from her little life. Gillian remains silent, though a smile is plastered on her lips. Our hands meet in the center console, slowly winding together as I drive as we listen to our little girl (*our little girl!*) wax poetic on everything she thinks I need to know about her.

When we get to Gillian's house, Stella finally yawns. "Okay, bedtime."

"Thank goodness," Gillian says under her breath.

We all get out of the car. Stella immediately gravitates

toward me and takes my hand. "Will you tuck me in, Daddy?"

"Of course, I will," I say. I glance over at Gillian. "Your mom might need to help me with the getting ready part, but–"

"No, no. You'll tuck me in. Just you and me, please," Stella says, one of the politest demands I've ever heard.

"Uh–"

Gillian laughs. "She knows everything she has to do. You just wait for her to climb into bed and ask for a story, alright?"

I nod, a bit dazed. I'm not prepared. I wasn't ready to be thrown into the deep end this fast.

"And if you need me, you just holler."

"He won't!" Stella exclaims.

We all head inside, Stella leading me straight back to her room. Gillian is right, she knows just what to do. She puts on her pajamas by herself, throws her clothes in the hamper, and brushes her teeth in the bathroom. Then, finally, she leaps into bed and pulls the blankets up to her chest, smiling at me. "Okay, I'm ready."

I nervously sit on the edge of the bed. "You're still wearing your necklace."

She frowns and touches the pendant around her neck. "Of course, I am. You have to be with me all the time."

My heart flutters. This kid is the most special little wonder I've ever met. And she's mine. Still can't wrap my mind around it. "Well, should I read you a story?"

Stella yawns and leans back further into her pillows. "Can we just talk?"

I glance back at her bedroom door that's cracked slightly. "Um..."

"This is my baby blanket," she says without waiting for

an answer, holding up the blanket on top of her. "Auntie Amy made it for me."

It's crocheted, with different patches creating a pastel rainbow.

"I sleep with it every night."

"It looks very cozy," I reply.

"Mhm. It is." She looks around the room, lit only by a warm orange lamp on her side table. "Daddy?"

I shimmy closer to her, tucking the blanket up to her chest again. "What is it, Stella?"

"Why didn't I know you were my daddy until now?" she asks. There is no judgment in her voice. Just bewilderment.

I want more than anything to call out for Gillian right now so she can help me navigate these tumultuous waters. But Stella wanted me to be here with her. Just me and her. We need all the alone time we can get after so many years of no time at all. "Well, I didn't know you were my baby, sweetie."

"That's strange," she says, pulling at one of the corners of her blanket. "Did Mommy know?"

I don't want to lie to the kid. And I don't want to make things more complicated than they already are. Still... "She did."

"Why didn't she tell you?"

"Well, it's complicated."

Stella blinks at me. Nothing is too complicated for this kid, I guess.

"Mommy and I...we cared for each other very much a long time ago. And things got in the way of us being together. So, when she found out she was having you, she didn't know how to tell me."

"That's sad."

I nod. "It is sad. But it's not Mommy's fault. So don't be mad at her, alright?"

Stella shrugs. "I'm not mad. I'm just happy you're here."

"I'm happy I'm here too." I run my hand through her hair. Her eyes flutter shut, a look of peace on her face. "And I promise I'm always going to be here for you."

Stella sighs blissfully. I can tell she's fading fast. I lean down and kiss her forehead. "Goodnight, my baby."

"Goodnight, my Daddy."

I smile and admire her one last moment. Her chest rises and falls heavily. Already drifting away. It's been a long day for my little girl. Finally, I turn off the light and tiptoe out of the bedroom.

Gillian is waiting for me just outside the door, a placid smile on her face. "Already out?"

"Like a light," I reply, closing the door behind me. I lean up against the wall and look down at her. "Were you listening?"

She shrugs. "Wanted to make sure I was here in case you needed me."

I half-laugh and loop my arms around her, pulling her hips softly to mine. "Funny thing about that is that I always need you."

"Oh really?" Gillian teases and then raises up on her tiptoes to kiss me.

"Really," I reply, heat rising in my cheeks.

Gillian plays with the hair at the base of my skull, gazing up at me. She truly is the most beautiful woman in the world. "You were so good with her."

"You think?"

She nods emphatically. "Yes. So amazing. You're such a good dad."

That clobbers me over the head with a wave of emotion I didn't expect. "Oh. Wow."

"Don't you feel it?" Gillian asks.

I shake my head. "I feel like I have a bit more to prove before I should be given such a compliment."

"No, honey. Not at all. It's ingrained in you. It's what you are."

I still can't believe it myself. But I'll try my best to let her words sink in.

Gillian kisses me again. A long, chaste kiss. Except her hands are grabbing onto me tighter than a chaste kiss should allow. When she pulls away, she looks up at me, eyes plaintive and suggesting more.

I cup her face in one hand, my thumb aligned with her jawbone, and kiss her once more. Our lips lock together just the same, except this time, my tongue sneaks between her lips, inviting myself deeper.

She moans against my mouth as quietly as she can and presses her body to mine. Flush against her, I can feel her pulsing heartbeat and the heat coming off of her sex.

It's making me hard.

Without words, we continue to kiss, although a sort of gravity pulls us down the hall toward Gillian's room. It is not loud and crashing like it would have been in our youth or even just a month ago. It is sensual, soft, and delicate.

As soon as we are behind the closed door of her bedroom, I pull her dress up over her head, exposing her beautiful body to the air. Goosebumps appear on every inch of her bare flesh. I begin to kiss every square inch of her body starting with her neck, working to her shoulders, to her chest...

Gillian whimpers and sinks down onto the bed further and further until she's sprawled out for me to devour.

When I reach her stomach, her hips buck up toward my mouth. I lift my head and smile at her. "Want something?"

"Axel, don't tease me," she murmurs. Her legs hook around my back. "I need you."

Those three words are all that need to be said. I pull her panties off, breathe in the scent of her musk, and then hungrily push my lips against her lower ones. She's so wet, the juices flow onto my tongue easily.

Gillian's body seizes as my tongue and lips devour her. I love to watch her squirm, how the pleasure spreads over every inch of her body. She grabs onto anything that she can find, rocking her hips into my chin.

I lock my lips around her swollen clit, relishing the gasp she lets out, before breaking away. "How do you want me to make you come, Gill?"

She breathes heavily, unable to answer me.

I lower my lips to the inside of her thigh. "You want to come on my tongue?"

"No...no, I want you inside when I come." Gillian reaches out for me, grabbing tight to the collar of my shirt. "Come here. I need you here."

I crawl up the length of her body and welcome her lips on mine once again. As we kiss, Gillian undoes the buttons on my shirt and then my pants. "Get naked for me, Axel. Let me feel all of you."

I shake off the shirt, then slide my pants off, casting it all to the side, leaving Gillian and me in complete naked bliss together. I run my hands down the sides of her beautiful body, admiring how my cock rests against her pelvis, waiting to be welcomed inside. Something feels different this time. We've had sex many times in all sorts of positions. Surely, missionary in her bed shouldn't feel more special.

Yet, it does.

"What are you waiting for?" she asks breathlessly.

I shake my head. "Nothing, just taking it all in."

Gillian smiles, eyelids lowered lustily. "I'd like to take *you* all in."

I snort, "Good one, Gill."

She wriggles her hips. "Please. Inside me now."

I would like to make Gillian happy the rest of my life. It's only natural I'd give into her in every possible way. I lean over her and position my cock at her entrance. I push my hips forward and try to ignore my pleasure to make sure I'm not hurting her.

Gillian's eyes flutter shut, head bending back. Her neck strains. "Oh god..."

"Is that okay?"

"Yes, yes, keep going."

I slide further into her, enjoying the tight welcoming grip of her pussy. "You feel so good," I mutter.

Gillian wraps her hand around the back of my neck, pressing her forehead to mine. "I love how you feel inside of me."

The word love, while not used in a necessarily romantic way, strikes a chord inside of me. The feeling has been growing not just weeks, but years between us. And I want her to feel my love in every possible way. With an even rhythm, I thrust my hips inside her, watching how her pleasure melts and shifts across her body.

Gillian grabs onto my ass and pushes me deeper. "All the way, baby."

"You drive me crazy, you know that?" I murmur in her ear.

She laughs, wrapping her arms around my back and legs around my hips. "Just want every inch."

"I'll give you all that and more."

"Promise?" she whispers.

I kiss the hinge of her jaw. "Promise with a capital 'p', Gillian."

We both go silent as we meld together, the slickness clicking between us. She's always felt amazing, but my heart is now desperately involved in this dance.

We are making love. It really feels like that. Needy hands grabbing onto one another for dear life, breath synced together, and the way our lips continue to come together for desperate moments of passion.

Something unlocks inside me. I start to pulse my hips faster. Gillian moans. I can't help it, it's biology. "Oh god," I whisper.

"Yes, keep going."

"Oh *my god*."

Gillian's hips collide with mine, just as desperate, her breaths aspirating with a growing whine.

"Look at me," I grunt. "Look in my eyes when you come."

Gillian's fiery brown eyes lock into mine, wide and full of fear.

"I've got you, mama. I've got you. Let go, I've..."

Gillian's chin tilts back. She gulps for the air. She's shaking beneath me, fingernails digging into my back. "I'm–I'm–"

I feel her come before she says anything, her pussy clenching tightly around me, pulsing with life. She keens into my shoulder, trying to mute her cry. "That's it," I whisper. "That's –" I feel the urge inside me that I'm about to release and ride her harder until I join her in a tremendous release. I drop my head into the bed and groan loudly.

Gillian's fingers twiddle through my hair. "That felt so good," she says. "You make me feel so..." she trails off, almost like her next words are held under lock and key. "Axel..."

"What is it, Gillian?" I ask, finally getting the strength to rise up onto my elbow and look her in the eye.

The face of the woman I love is strained with fear.

"What is it?"

"I'm scared."

I brush her sweated hair out of her face. "Why are you scared, baby? Tell me."

"Because–because –"

Holy shit. She's about to beat me to the punch. I thought I would be the first to say it. In fact, I planned for it. At first, it scared me, but now I crave it.

"I..."

No. I'm going to say it first. I'm going to save her the fear.

"I love you," we both utter at the same time. A smile spreads across my face as her eyes widen with recognition that we've just taken the words out of each other's mouths. Then she smiles too.

"I love you," I repeat. Then, I pepper kisses over her face, saying it again and again.

"Axel!" she squeals, pushing me back so we can lock eyes. "Let me say it."

I swallow.

"I love you," Gillian says definitively. It is a fact that will not be questioned. "I've loved you for seven years."

My jaw drops.

"Longer than that. I think I was born to love you, Axel."

"Oh, Gillian..." I shake my head in disbelief.

"It's corny, I know, but–"

"No, I feel the same way." I trail my fingers down from her face to her body, landing right at her stomach. I missed the most important part of our love story. Our baby growing inside of her. There is not only a hollowness to knowing I've missed out on Stella's life, but also knowing I missed out on our love growing for her together. Before she was born.

As if reading my mind, Gillian presses my hand to her belly. "You're here now, Axel. That's more than I ever thought I'd have."

I kiss her once more. "And I'm never going anywhere, baby. I'm here. Forever. You're stuck with me."

Gillian giggles. "You're the best possible person I could be stuck with."

"Promise?"

She touches my cheek, making sure our eyes are locked. "I promise. You are the love of my life, Axel."

I draw her into my arms and push my face into her neck. I have no words, just actions.

I will spend the rest of my life making sure Gillian knows that I'm always here for her. And for Stella.

No matter what.

29

GILLIAN

ONE MONTH LATER...

THE WARM WATER RUNS OVER MY SHOULDER AND CHEST as I press the bottom of my foot against the glass shower door as Axel presses himself inside me. "Oh god," I whisper.

He bites down on his upper lip, an effective gag so he doesn't moan too loudly.

I hug my arms around his neck tightly and push my face against his slick neck. The shower water continues to wash over us, making the communion of our bodies that much more intense. In the heat of July, it's one of the only ways we don't get sweaty while having sex.

Not that I mind the sweat. However, a shower plus sex kills two birds with one stone.

Axel tilts my chin back and hungrily kisses me, his plush ruby lips caressing mine. His tongue lashes into my mouth; I can't help but groan and lash back.

His hands slide down to my ass, grabbing all that he can, forcing our parts together so tightly I'm not sure he can go any deeper. I squeal at the pleasure and immediately throw my hand against my mouth.

Axel stops and looks me in the eye warily. "Careful..."

"Couldn't help it," I whisper. Stella is downstairs with Lola, but who knows where that little girl wanders off to sometimes? Better safe than sorry.

He smiles back at me, taking the moment to catch his breath, chest heaving up and down. His hair is completely wet, sending rivers of water down his neck. "Can you handle it, Gill?"

"I can handle it. Now, hurry up, we don't have much time," I murmur.

Axel starts to laugh, but I cut him off with a kiss. The clock is counting down quicker than I'd like and I want to get an orgasm in before I get ready.

Luckily, with Axel, I can always count on that.

Axel pins my hands against the wall and drops his mouth to my collarbone, nipping and sucking. I bite the inside of my cheek and make sure to take measured breaths. It's getting harder to stay quieter as his cock drives deep into me, even *harder* when he starts twisting one of my nipples between his fingers.

"Fuck, fuck, fuck, Axel," I mutter as quietly as I can.

"Shhh."

"Fuck you."

He laughs and begins to thrust his hips harder.

I rest my head against the shower wall, relishing the water as it rushes over my face, just as I feel pleasure starting to run through my veins. "Oh," I gasp. "Oh, oh, oh." I pulse my hips with each utterance, the last one coming out strained and high pitched.

Axel pounds into me, huffing like a wild animal against my shoulder.

I put my fist in my mouth and bite down just in time. An orgasm snaps inside me, somehow pulling Axel deeper.

The fist works as a perfect buffer for my trembling whimper of pleasure.

Axel claps his hands against my ass and thrusts just twice more before he comes, pressing his lips tightly together so the guttural groan is contained.

I push my mouth against his ear, let him hear my heavy breaths as we both come down from the height of pleasure. The only sound for a few moments is the water rushing down the shower walls. Axel rests his forearms on the wall along either side of my head and kisses my cheek, slowly, longingly.

I run my hands up and down his sides, muscles slick with water and soap residue. "Mmm...let's do that again," I say.

Axel chuckles and kisses the side of my head before sliding out of me, his cock growing soft. "Have to save some for later, Gillian."

The trick with us is we never save anything for later because it's *constant*. The need...the desire...I feel it all the time. I pout my lower lip out. "Ax..."

"Don't pout. We've got a party to get to. Come on."

Axel steps out of the shower before I can stop him, reaching for a towel and wrapping it around himself.

I stay there against the wall, catching my breath for a moment. I let my eyes close and sigh. Just a month and everything has changed. I've gone from a single mother to a *not* so single mother. And Axel has gone from a bachelor to a father. It can get overwhelming at times. But when we have each other...

I'm stunned back to reality when Axel knocks on the glass shower door.

"I'm coming!" I cry out.

"You don't look like you're coming!" he cries back.

"Is that a double entendre?"

He lets out a loud laugh. "Maybe."

I grin.

***

"Okay, I'm ready, I'm ready," I call out as I put my second earring in.

"Finally!" Stella chimes.

I laugh to myself as I go join them in the living room, now deemed the toy room as evidenced by how Stella has commandeered it (with a special thanks to Axel who has gone way overboard in spoiling her). "Did Daddy tell you to say that?" I ask, putting my hands on my hips and surveying the scene.

Stella is sitting on the floor putting together a racetrack for her Hot Wheels with Lola while Axel sits fixing his cuff in an armchair. The television plays in the background, already on the five o'clock news. We were supposed to be out of the house at four-forty-five to make it to Kira's birthday dinner out in Malibu on time. Of course the one time my sister actually *wants* to celebrate her birthday with a party, I'd like to just curl up at home with the two people I love most in the world.

"What do you think?" Lola replies, eyeing her brother.

I look over at Axel who grins, but doesn't look up at me, still fixated on his cufflink. Before I can respond, I'm distracted by the television.

"The struggle over the Seton lot has finally ended, as evidenced by this morning's groundbreaking."

I smile as I watch the screen that focuses on a bulldozer pulling up a patch of earth. The decision didn't even need to be left to the city council once Axel brought his plans to the board at Stella's school. Both parties agreed to drop the whole thing and leave it to Hitchins. So far, he's made good on every promise regarding the development.

The camera switches to an image of Jeremiah, hard hat and all, smiling as he speaks to an interviewer. "We're so proud to be able to bring the community together and make some good in the Silver Lake area. We hope to continue making good all across LA and even have plans to reconfigure an old development in Echo Park to be a beneficial community space."

I glance at Axel who is now watching the television with a look of pride. He managed to bring Jeremiah back into the fold at Hitchins, which took some work on both sides. However, with Axel's father taking more of a step back from the company and Axel wanting to establish a Community Care division, everyone now seems satisfied.

Axel's now in talks to develop some properties with the Ricks Group. Turns out the positive press has been more of a boon than anyone could have imagined.

"Alright, are you ready to go, dear?" Axel asks, getting to his feet.

"Let's do it," I say.

Lola taps Stella on the shoulder. "Time to say goodbye, kiddo."

Stella hops to her feet and gives me a quick hug. "Bye, Mommy." Then, she rushes over to Axel and bounds into his arms. "BYE, DADDY!"

Axel catches her and swings her around. "Bye, kiddo!"

I cross my arms and shake my head, mostly as a joke. "What am I, chopped liver?"

Lola laughs. "She's just used to you."

"I'm old news."

"That's not what I said," she replies, eyeing me playfully. I'm so grateful Lola and I have been able to remain as close as ever, if not closer. Now, there are no lies. And I don't think there will be any more ever again. "You look perfect, Gill."

I scoff. "Oh, this old thing?" I pull up the skirt of my dress. It's brand new. A mustard yellow dress with a tie waist that reveals one of my legs. Shows you what he likes. "Axel got it for me," I say, trying not to blush.

Lola just smiles and shakes her head. What's that about?

"Thanks for watching Stella tonight."

"Any time, you know it," Lola says with a firm nod.

"Okay, gotta go," Axel says to Stella, giving her a big smooch on the side of the head. "Love you."

"Love you more!" Stella chirps as he sets her down.

"No, I love you more."

"No, I –"

"I love you both more than either of you could possibly love each other," I cry out. "Now, come on or we'll be here all day."

Axel rushes over to me and grabs me by the hand. We both cry out a few more goodbyes and "I love yous" to Stella as we go out the door, beaming all the way to the car.

Once we're settled inside, I expect Axel to turn on the car and peel out of the driveway at top speed. But for a second, he just sits. Takes a breath. Gives me a moment to admire him. Dark hair, those eyes I'd like to get lost in as if it's the densest forest in all the world, cheekbones as sharp as diamonds.

The silence ends with Axel taking a deep breath and dropping his hands on the steering wheel. "Alright, ready?"

His eyes meet mine and I can't help but smile. "Ready."

I KNOW something is up when we hit Malibu and Axel says he's lost.

"What do you mean, you're lost? It's the PCH. You just drive," I say, gesturing the sprawling beachfront highway.

"Where is the place again?" he asks.

"Pull over."

Axel does so while I open the family text and scroll through for the name of the restaurant. "Paulo's. It should be–" I look up for the cross street and then back at the image of the map in the group text. "Wait. It says it should be here, but that's not possible because..."

I look around. I know this spot. I've been here many times before.

This is where we park for our spot. The cove of the beach.

"What's going on?" I frown and look at Axel.

He doesn't seem to be confused. In fact, he's smiling. "They must have given us the wrong directions."

"I...I'll text them." I send off a text quickly and then stare at my phone, waiting for someone, anyone to reply.

Nothing.

"You've got to be kidding," I mutter.

"It's okay. They'll get back to us."

I put my phone in my lap and look around. "Well. Guess we just wait."

Axel glances out at the beach. "You want to go for a quick walk to our spot?"

I shake my head. "I won't get service out there."

"It'll be quick."

I huff. It's my own fault that we're late but it's not my fault we're lost. That can fall squarely on Kira's shoulders.

"Axel, I really just want to get this figured out before we–"

"Hey..." he says softly and takes my hand.

Something about his touch is so soft and something about his eyes is so urging I'm not sure I can fight him anymore.

"Just do this with me, Gillian."

This is...something's going on.

Oh my god. Is this *the* something? The something that would be crazy it was happening because we've only been back together for a month and it'd be crazy for him to ask and even crazier for me to say yes, but I know I would in a heartbeat?

No way. Right?

"Alright."

Axel and I get out of the car and kick off our shoes before walking carefully down the beach. "The water's too high," I say. "My dress –"

Before I can say anything more, Axel sweeps me off my feet into his arms. I squeal. "Axel!"

"I'll carry you."

Axel carries me until it's safe for me to walk on my own. I round the rocky outcrop, almost expecting the cove to be decorated with candles and rose petals.

However, there's nothing.

Gillian, you're crazy.

I walk into the middle of the cove and sigh. "Okay. Here we are. Romantic, isn't it?" I say through a chuckle.

Axel doesn't respond.

"Sorry, I know I'm being a little bit of a pill. We're just already late and I want to–" I turn back around to face Axel and am stunned to find him on bended knee before me. He's holding a ring box. *It's happening.* "Oh my god."

"You nearly ruined a good surprise, Gillian," Axel says with a broad smile.

I put my hand to my lips. "What are you doing?"

"What does it look like?"

I stare at him.

"Do you...want me to stop?" he asks nervously.

"No, no, don't stop."

Axel laughs at himself. "Okay. Good. That'd be awkward. Um...I had a whole thing memorized, but now that I'm here with you, my mind has gone blank."

I smile, my eyes starting to well with tears.

"This has been our spot for a long time. Even when we didn't come here together, I always thought of this as our spot. We might have spent a long time apart, but you never left my heart, Gillian." Axel gulps, trying his best not to let his anxiety show through his smile. I know him too well, though, I can see it. "You've given me so much love and kindness since we were kids. You've given me a child who even after just a month, I can't imagine my life without."

My smile is so big it's hurting my cheeks.

"And after just a month of being with you, I know I need to be with you for a lifetime." He opens the ring box, revealing an emerald set on a gold band. Stella's birth stone. Same color as their eyes. "Will you marry me?"

"Yes. Yes. Of course. Yes."

Axel starts to reach for my hand, but I drop to my knees, not caring if my new dress gets dirty. Who cares when I'm literally a second away from being engaged?! I put my hand out for him and wriggle my ring finger. "This one."

"Thank god, I was definitely going to have to ask."

I laugh hard as he slides the ring onto my finger. I can't even believe my eyes.

"Do you like it?"

I wrap my hands around the sides of Axel's head and kiss him with everything I have in me. "Love it. Love it so much. Love *you* so much."

Axel wraps his arms around me and kisses me again. "I love you more, pretty sure."

"Oh no, not this again..." I groan. Then, I remember. "Kira's birthday!"

Axel squints his eyes closed. "Gillian, that was a ploy."

"What?!" I should have known Kira hadn't turned over a new life and wanted a celebration all of a sudden.

"She wanted to make up for making things messy with Martin...and everything else. Although, I'm quite glad she did," Axel says before kissing me right on the nose.

"This is the best day of my life!"

I jump to attention when I hear Stella's voice. From the dune grass, she emerges, beaming from ear to ear. She skips over and squeezes in between us. "How did you get here?!" I ask in shock.

"Lola drove me."

"At the speed of light?" I gape.

Stella wasn't the only one hiding in the dune grass. My sisters all emerge, Grant, baby Tana, Lola and Jeremiah, and, of course, Dad.

I feel drowned in love as they all crowd around us, celebrating our engagement. Hugs, kisses, tears. I don't even know what to do with myself.

They've also brought a picnic for us all to share. We spend the evening reveling in Axel and my love. Stella sits between us grinning from ear to ear. I don't need to be right next to Axel to know that my love for him is as boundless as the Pacific or grains of sand on the beach.

"Can I see the ring?" Stella eventually asks.

I hold my hand out and show her, then hold it up next

to her face. "It's the same color as your eyes." It's not painful anymore to see Axel's eyes in Stella's. It's my favorite thing in the world. I look up at Axel with a smile. "Both of your eyes."

Axel smiles back and wraps his arms around Stella. "What do you think? Did I do a good job?"

And just that image right there, two green-eyed loves of my life, brings me to tears. I embrace them, give them kisses, and bask in the way they both whisper, "I love you."

I never knew my heart could be so full it's overflowing.

EPILOGUE
AXEL

I lean back in the chair and stare out at the ocean, placid blue extending for miles and miles and miles.

My stomach is twisting in knots. My suit feels itchy. Too tight and constricting, even though it's made of linen. I run my hands back through my hair and then curse, remembering I've already coiffed it in the mirror. Can't help being antsy.

I'm starting to regret this. Not the marrying Gillian part. But have a major spectacle of a wedding.

It was my idea to get married in Maldives. I wanted to marry her in style. Wanted to show off just how much I loved her by screaming it to the world and making sure every last person heard it. Which is how I've ended up in a tropical paradise with over a hundred of our closest friends and family waiting to watch me and Gill get married.

On Christmas Eve, no less. That was Stella's idea. And if there's one thing I've learned about myself in the past six months since becoming a father, it's that I will do anything for my little girl.

Including planning a wedding to her exact date specifications.

Gillian always says I'm spoiling her. I just tell her I've got years of catching up to do.

I feel a hand on my shoulder. "You're freaking out, aren't you?"

I flip around to face Lola. "What are you doing here?! Shouldn't you –"

"Grant came to get me," my sister says with a sympathetic smile. "Said you needed a pep talk."

I glance over her shoulder to catch a glimpse of Grant through the cottage where me and the groomsmen were getting ready. He smiles to himself and then disappears. He really has become a good friend. Knew exactly what I needed. My sister.

Jeremiah has been helpful too, but he doesn't know Gillian like Lola does. Lola is practically Gillian's other half.

"You look great," I say, getting to my feet. Her vibrant yellow dress brings out the green in her eyes.

She grins. "So do you. Let me just..." She starts to redistribute strands of my hair.

I try to duck away. "*Moooommmm.*"

"Relax, I'm trying to help you. You don't want Gillian to run away, do you?"

"Is that a possibility?!" It's not, right?

Lola rolls her eyes. "God, you're such an idiot."

"I'm about to get married. I'm allowed to be an idiot."

Her hands settle on my arms. "Axel. You'll be fine. Gillian's not going to run away."

I chew on my lower lip. "Is she excited?"

Lola squeezes. "Of course."

"Good. Okay. Good."

"What are you afraid of, Axel?"

I shake my head. "Snakes, for starters."

"You're such a *dad*, oh my god," she says, slapping me on the arm. Then she starts to tinker with my tie and straightening out the brightly colored tropical flower on my lapel. "You have literally been working toward this moment for like a decade."

I quirk an eyebrow. "What do you mean?"

Lola laughs. "Don't you get it? You and Gillian were literally made for each other. It's obvious."

"You think so?" Because I feel the truth of that statement in my soul.

My sister smiles. Lola has been our biggest champion since everything played out this past summer. She likes to lord the betrayal of her only rule over both of us from time to time, but it's always with a sly grin. Plus, she got Stella out of it and I know *none* of us would trade that.

"Axel —" Grant calls out from the cottage, poking his head out. "Time for us to head out."

My heart drops into my stomach. But only for a moment. Because Lola grabs my hand and whispers, "Don't you dare be nervous. This is the beginning of everything for you."

I feel like I'm on autopilot up until I make it up to the altar under a canopy of flowers. The heat has broken for the evening, but I'm still feeling like sweat is beading across my forehead.

I nervously scan the guests though my eyes can't seem to focus on any of their faces until I clap eyes on my dad who is sitting in the first row, looking grumpy as usual.

Things haven't been the same since I wriggled the company out from under his iron fist. And that's a good thing. For once, I think he's considering retirement. And he's getting his health in order, something that was never a priority to him before.

Being a grandfather was like a reset for him. Knowing that there was someone to live for beyond his children, to watch grow up and become their own person, softened him.

Still, he looks like the grumpy guy he's been since Mom passed. But when he sees me looking at him, he sticks his thumb up and gives me a nod.

Thanks, Dad. And I mean it.

The bridal party starts to walk down the aisle. All of Gillian's sisters, my friends, capped off with my siblings: Lola, the maid of honor and Jeremiah, my best man. Jeremiah squeezes my arm once he's set in position beside me. "You got this, man."

I've been preparing all day for the moment I see Gillian walk down the aisle, but I didn't prepare enough to see Stella in her little white dress with a basket full of flower petals arriving at the end of the aisle. When her eyes land on me, she smiles brighter than I've ever seen. Gillian's smile, a copy and paste.

I hold my breath as she walks toward me. Her basket runs out slightly before she makes it to the end of the aisle. I can see the disappointment in her eyes. "Stella," I say in order to distract her.

She looks to me and skips over, throwing her arms around my waist. I embrace her, all the guests cooing sweetly at the image.

Then the music shifts. Our song, 'Witchcraft', played with string instruments.

I keep Stella at my side, though we rehearsed that she'd

go take her seat in the front row next to my dad. I can't bear to let her go right now.

My heart is racing as the white curtains are pulled aside to reveal Gillian.

Though she's flanked by Kent and Dana, she may as well be the only other person in the world. Like a spotlight is positioned on her. Gillian glows, and it's not just because her skintight dress is covered in beads that look like constellations cascading down her curves.

She's always glowed. Since we were kids.

Our eyes meet. All the nerves fall away.

This is all exactly right. Just as it was supposed to be.

"Daddy, you're crying," Stella whispers, tucking her chin against my hip and looking up at me.

I smile, though tears are streaming down my cheeks. "Yeah, you're right. I think I am."

She buries her face in my leg and watches with me as our life as a family comes closer and closer to fruition.

Gillian's hair is pulled back and decorated with flowers that match the ones in my lapel, pearls dangling from her ears like dewdrops, and eyes glimmering with tears that match mine.

Takes everything in me not to run up and embrace her. But I wait. Soon enough, I'll have her in my arms, every day, for the rest of my life.

Dana gives Gillian a hug and a kiss before coming to me. "Take care of her, alright?" she asks, lip trembling. She runs her hand through Stella's hair. "Both of them."

"Of course," I reply.

Dana kisses my cheek, then steps over to the bridesmaids.

All that's left before Gillian's hands are in mine is her father giving her away.

Kent's already got a Maldivian tan, making his white smile effervescent. He's not shedding tears yet. *Yet*.

He leads Gillian toward me and places her hand in mine. Sparks fly through my body, the potential energy of what's about to happen becoming *real*. Kent clasps our hands in his. "You two, be good."

"No promises, Dad," Gillian grins.

Kent pats her cheek tenderly and then sighs, bringing his gaze toward me.

I nod. "Y-yes."

"Then she's yours," Kent says.

Gillian doesn't balk even a little bit at the undercurrents of antiquity, the dated practice of her father giving her away to me. It's not like that at all anyway. Gillian is wild and free like the ocean, like the wind. If I get to bathe in her waters, bask in her breezes, I will be the luckiest man on earth.

Kent takes Stella by the hand, leading her down to her seat, leaving Gillian and me under the canopy. Finally.

"You look amazing," I whisper.

"So do you," she says back.

"No, but you look..."

Gillian stops me, squeezing my hands. Her engagement ring presses against one of my fingers. "We look amazing."

"We look..." I chuckle. "Yeah."

The ceremony is all very standard. The usual introductions and readings. However, once it gets to the vows, things are a little unconventional.

Jeremiah, keeper of the rings, passes one ring to Gillian and two to me.

Gillian frowns. "Two? Isn't that a little overkill?"

I shake my head. "Not at all. Stella, can you come up here, honey?"

Stella looks to Kent for approval and, once she has it, carefully creeps up to the altar.

"Stand with your mother, would you?"

"What are you doing?" Gillian asks with a nervous smile.

I clear my throat. "I have a few vows for Stella before I vow myself to you, if that's okay with you?"

She nods, and I can see she is both curious and proud that I chose to include our daughter in the ceremony.

"Stella, with this ring, I vow to you that I will always love you. I'll always cherish you and be here for you. To protect you, to play with you, to hear you, to be whatever you want me to be, whenever you need me to be. I love you, my little star, and this..." I point at her and then myself, "...is forever and a day."

I slide the ring onto Stella's little finger.

"It matches my necklace!" Stella remarks, twiddling her fingers to show off the diamond set in a star shape on her finger.

"You got it," I reply with a smile.

"I love you, Daddy."

"I love you too, baby."

After kissing her forehead, I nod to the officiant.

The officiant smiles and reads off the official vows. The ones I'm more than glad to take. The ones that will bind me to the love of my life forever. "With this ring..."

"With this ring..." I repeat.

We go like this, back and forth, me repeating after the officiant that I will live to honor and love Gillian for the rest of my life.

Stella is tucked against the front of Gillian's dress, smiling up at me.

Gillian's tears start to tumble. As she recites the same vow back to me, each word wobbles.

Everything feels real once she slides the wedding ring onto my finger. Our hands entangle together.

And when I hear those words, "I now pronounce you husband and wife," I am unable to restrain myself.

I kiss Gillian deeply and utterly with every piece of my soul. Then, the two of us hoist Stella into the air, planting matching kisses on her cheeks. She laughs. "Gross!"

"Oh, you love it," Gillian razzes, patting Stella's belly. Then, her eyes find mine. "Best day ever."

That's what every day on our journey has felt like. The days just get better.

"It's my great honor to announce, Mr. and Mrs. Hitchins!"

"And Stella Hitchins!" Stella announces proudly, her arm locked around my neck.

I can't afford to shed even one more tear. Especially not with a smile so wide on my face. "My girls...has a nice ring to it, huh?"

"I like it," Gillian says. "What do you think, Stell?"

Stella lifts her head proudly. "Sounds just right to me."

We don't just walk down the aisle as man and wife. We walk down as a family.

Doesn't get better than that.

ALSO BY CALLIE STEVENS

The Hawthorns Series

Baby For Daddy's Best Friend

Baby For The Off Limits Single Daddy

Secret Daddy Next Door

Baby For The Off Limits Boss Daddy

The Solace Sisters Series

Silver Fox's Secret Baby

Enemy Ex's Secret Baby

Enemy Daddy Next Door

Faux Beau's Baby Surprise

Enemy Boss's Baby Surprise

Alpha Billionaire Daddies

Damaged Secret Daddy

Fake Fiancé Boss Daddy

Broken Single Daddy's Baby

Spades Brothers Series

Accidental Baby For My Brother's Best Friend

Accidental Secret Daddy

Secret Baby For My Best Friends Brother

Baby For My Best Friend's Ex

Soul Sounds Brothers

Stuck With My Rockstar Boss

Unexpected Baby For My Brother's Best Friend

Accidental Fake Fiancé

Claimed By My Best Friend's Brother